Secret Wishes

Other Avon Camelot Books by
Lou Kassem

MIDDLE SCHOOL BLUES

LOU KASSEM is a fourth-generation daughter of the mountains of eastern Tennessee who says she has always "told stories." For years before becoming a published writer, she wrote plays, stories, and monologues for her four daughters and their friends, for schools, and for civic and church groups. "The laughter and tears associated with growing up have always fascinated me," she says. "The problems may be centuries old, but each child is different." When not writing, her favorite pastimes are reading, playing golf, traveling, and talking to young people about books and writing. Lou Kassem and her husband live in Blacksburg, Virginia. She is the author of the Avon Camelot book *Middle School Blues*.

Secret Wishes

Lou Kassem

AN AVON CAMELOT BOOK

AVON BOOKS
A division of
The Hearst Corporation
105 Madison Avenue
New York, New York 10016

Copyright © 1989 by Lou Kassem
Published by arrangement with the author
Library of Congress Catalog Card Number: 88-92115
ISBN: 0-380-75544-0
RL: 5.9

First Avon Camelot Printing: February 1989

Printed in the U.S.A.

OPM 10 9 8 7 6 5 4 3 2 1

For everyone who ever had a secret wish

Contents

Chapter 1

Secrets

"You've hardly touched your breakfast, Margo."

"I'm full. I ate plenty, Mom."

"Wasting food is sinful. There are hungry people in the world who'd love to have what's left on your plate."

I sighed and picked up my fork. I just knew it would be like this. Mom had heaped my plate with scrambled eggs, sausages, fried apples, and toast.

"Hey, don't turn on the waterworks," Joel said. "I'll eat your sausage."

"I'll take the toast," offered Frank.

"Thanks, guys."

"No problem," Joel said. "We working men have to keep up our strength."

"Where do *you* work?"

"Didn't Mom tell you about our summer jobs? Boy, you go away for the summer and you forget everything. We're working for Green Thumb Lawns," Frank said.

"Yeah. And guess where we're going today?" Joel asked, giving me a sly smile.

"Where?"

"To your friend Brandy's. The Wines have been in Europe all summer. Boy, is their place amazing! Takes all day to mow and trim."

Brandy was no friend of mine and Joel knew it. "Maybe they'll like Europe so much they'll stay over there," I ventured.

Frank laughed. "Nice try, Margo. Your friend returns tomorrow."

"Great." I pushed my eggs around on my plate to make the pile seem smaller. The only thing Brandy and I had in common was that we were both new in town last year. Brandy has a smashing figure, piles of money, and is a first-class snob. It hadn't taken her long to draw a charmed circle of admirers around her. Fat Margo was not included. In fact, the only time Brandy and her crowd ever noticed me was when they needed someone to pick on . . . which usually happened at least once a day.

"Speaking of friends," Mom said, "Cindy wanted you to call her as soon as you got home. She said it was very important."

"Why didn't you tell me?"

"Because we didn't get home until after midnight. It's not even eight o'clock yet, Margo. You may call Cindy at a reasonable hour."

It was pointless to argue. I would have to wait.

A horn sounded out front. My brothers gulped the last of their breakfasts. "We'll be home after football practice," Joel called.

I washed the dishes and watched the clock.

2

Cindy Cunningham's my best friend. She isn't awed by Brandy's designer clothes, outrageous parties, or "in" clique. In fact, Cindy's the unofficial leader of the "un-in" crowd. She bubbles with energy and ideas. I could hardly wait to hear about her summer.

At one minute after nine I raced for the phone. "Hi, Cindy. I'm back. What's up?"

"Margo! You sure cut it close. How's your grandmother?"

"Oma's fine. She's walking again."

"That's great! Boy, am I glad you're home. Seems like you've been gone forever, not just three months."

"What all have I missed?"

Cindy laughed. "A great party, for one thing."

"Which party?"

"Becca and I had a back-to-school bash last Thursday. All our gang was back in town, except you. We had a fabulous time. At least most of us did. One person kinda moped around because you weren't there."

"Who?"

"That's my surprise."

"Come on, Cindy . . ."

"My lips are sealed. If you want the name of the Mystery Moper meet me at our lockers bright and early Monday morning."

Wild horses can't drag something out of Cindy she doesn't want to tell. "Okay," I said. "But I have a *little* surprise for you too."

"Is it bigger than a bread box?"

"Oh, yes. Definitely."

"Is it something to wear?"

3

"No."

"Something to eat?"

"No," I said, giggling.

She kept on asking questions until Mom said I'd been on the phone long enough. I promised to get to school early and hung up.

Cindy could have asked a zillion questions and never figured out my surprise. Thinking back, I could hardly believe what had happened myself. And it all began with a simple question.

"Did you ever have a secret wish, Margo? One that you never told anyone about?"

"Sure, Oma."

My grandmother and I were sitting on the front porch of the farmhouse, shelling the first peas of early summer. At least, Oma was shelling peas. I was watching her flying fingers put a constant green stream into the pan—zip ... plip ... plip ... plip. My peas were scattered all over the porch.

"I have a secret wish, too."

Something in her voice made me look up. Oma isn't your typical grandmother. She has more energy and enthusiasm than most people my age. If anyone could be two places at once—and enjoy it—it's Oma. Opa calls it her *spizerinktum*. Oma says she's just blessed with old-fashioned get-up-and-go. That's why it was so sad to see her stuck in a wheelchair. It's been almost a year since the car accident and her leg still hasn't healed properly.

"If you'll tell me your secret, I'll tell you mine," she offered.

"You'll think I'm stupid. You'll laugh."

4

"No, I won't. Try me."

"Better than that, I'll show you." I jumped up, planted my feet and put my hands on my hips. "Ready . . . Set . . . Give me a V . . . Give me an I . . . Give me a C . . . Give me a T . . . Give me an O . . . Give me an R . . . Give me a Y . . . V-I-C-T-O-R-Y . . . Victory! Victory! Ruffner, Ruffner!"

At the end of my cheer I jumped high into the air. Unfortunately, I landed off balance and ended up sprawled on the porch.

Oma *was* laughing.

Footsteps pounded toward us from inside the house. "What's all the commotion? Is somebody hurt?"

"No, Hannah. Margo was showing me a cheer."

Hannah's bulky body filled the doorway. She glared at me. "Your foolishness near 'bout gave me a heart attack, Margo. People have died of fright, you know." Holding her chest dramatically, she clumped back down the hall before I could apologize.

Oma was still chuckling. "Margo Wagner, you cheated. You meant to make me laugh."

"Of course I did. I like to make people laugh."

The smile vanished from Oma's face. "This is truly your secret wish? You want to be a cheerleader?"

I stood up and brushed some smashed peas from my shorts. "I've wanted to be a cheerleader for a long time—ever since Joel and Frank played sports in Little League. I learned all the cheers and all the moves but I was too fat to try out."

"You aren't fat now, Margo. You're only pleasingly plump."

5

"Plump is only good for pillows, Oma. Thin is in. Especially for cheerleaders."

"Stop making jokes, Margo," Oma ordered, "or I will think you are not serious about your wish."

I sat in my chair again and grabbed a handful of pea pods. "I'm serious, Oma. I'd like to be a cheerleader more than anything in the world. But that doesn't happen to girls like me."

"What do you mean by 'girls like you'?"

"Cheerleaders are special. They're always the prettiest, most co-ordinated, most popular girls in school."

"And you are none of these things?"

I knew Oma thought I was all of the above. Parents and grandparents are like that. But they aren't the ones who determine where you rank with your classmates. How could I hope to make her understand? "I've begun to fit in at Ruffner, Oma. I have some friends. I make good grades. But being a cheerleader's just a dream, I guess. What about you? What's your secret wish?"

Oma glanced at the screen door and rolled her wheelchair closer to me. "I want to walk again," she whispered.

Automatically, I looked down at her shrunken left leg. "B-but the doctor said—"

"Horsefeathers! Doctors know medicine. They don't know me." She dismissed the whole medical profession with a wave of her hand. "They may think at my age I should be content with my crutches and wheelchair, but I'm not. And for several months I've been doing something about it."

"What?"

"Exercises. The ones that physical therapist at

6

the hospital showed me. Only I've been doing twice the number she told me to do."

To demonstrate her point, Oma lifted her shriveled leg up and down four times. "See? My leg still works. I couldn't even do one lift at first."

"But it's shorter than your other leg."

"That's where you come in."

"Me?"

Oma nodded, her eyes twinkling with mischief. "If you'll help, I'll be out of this contraption by summer's end."

I didn't believe her but I said, "How can I help?"

Oma reached into her dress pocket and pulled out a creased paper. "While I was at the doctor's office for a check-up I found this ad in a magazine. Read it."

The ad from WALKRITE ORTHOPEDIC SHOES promised help for all foot, leg, and back problems.

"I wrote them," Oma said, barely giving me time to read the ad. "They can make me a built-up shoe for this sorry leg."

"Did you show this ad to Opa?"

Oma shook her head. "No! Horst thinks my fragile bones are safer in a wheelchair. I don't want to worry him—or my children—but I aim to try to walk again."

I'm soft-hearted. Everyone knows it—my brothers, my friends, and even the animals here on the farm. "What do you want me to do?"

Oma smiled and relaxed. "First, you'd better take these peas to Hannah so she can fix them for dinner. I'll tell you my plan when you come back."

I took the peas from Oma's lap and went to the

kitchen. Hannah wasn't there but already the tangy, tempting aroma of roasting pork and apples filled the air. I put the pan on the counter and began making some lemonade for Oma and me.

I was glad Hannah Schultz was busy elsewhere. It wasn't that I didn't like her. Opa was lucky to find someone to cook and clean for Oma after she came home from the hospital. No, the trouble with Hannah is that she collects troubles. Misery—hers and other people's—is her favorite topic of conversation. She has a horror story for every occasion. It can be very depressing. Just the other day Hannah had told us—in gory detail—about two car accidents, a friend who was dying of cancer, and a farmer who was going bankrupt.

One night Opa made the mistake of saying, "Miss Hannah's a godsend."

Oma snapped, "I'd just as soon God send her somewhere else!"

Then she told Opa about our daily dose of misery and we all laughed.

I put the pitcher of lemonade and two glasses on a tray and went back to the porch.

"Sit here close to me and I'll tell you what I have in mind," Oma said. "After Hannah leaves this afternoon I want you to measure my foot. Then we'll fill out the order in your name and send off for the shoes."

"Why in my name?"

"Because our postman, that Ira Hopkins, is a nosy old gossip. Everybody in the county would know what I was up to. He won't suspect a package for you. Especially if you mail the order in town.

8

There's no sense in everyone knowing our business. And while we're waiting for the shoes you can help me with my exercising."

"I don't know anything about exercising."

"It's really quite simple," Oma reassured me. "While I'm supposed to be sleeping every afternoon we'll exercise and practice walking with that new shoe. By summer's end we'll surprise everyone, including Dr. Baumgartner."

I was beginning to have serious doubts. This project didn't sound simple to me. "Shouldn't you listen to what your doctor tells you?"

"I am, Margo. Dr. Baumgartner said with intensive therapy I *might* be able to walk again. He and your grandpa just think I'm too old. And maybe this shoe will do the trick. It's worth a try. Will you help me?"

Against my better judgment, I nodded.

Oma settled back in her wheelchair with a satisfied sigh. "Now let's see about your secret wish. I don't know much about cheerleaders, except for those Dallas girls on TV. But it strikes me, with all that jumping and prancing, they must be in good physical condition. Right?"

"Uh-huh."

"Pigs say 'uh-huh,' Margo."

"Yes, ma'am. Cheerleaders needed to be in very good shape."

Oma looked me up and down. "Well then, I'd say our first job is to get you tuned up."

"How?" She didn't realize it but getting me to look anything like the Dallas Cowboy Cheerleaders was more impossible than her walking again.

9

"When you walk into town tomorrow to mail the letter, stop by the library. Check out some of those fitness books. Get a diet book and a nutrition book, too. From what I hear on those morning TV talk shows, if you're going to get in shape you need to do it properly."

"Did you say *walk* into town? It's more than three miles, each way."

Oma's eyes twinkled. "Part of your conditioning program, Margo. It won't kill you. I used to walk farther than that to school every morning. It's time to start exercising. Nothing comes easy, you know."

"Okay, I'll give it a try," I said grudgingly. "But I'll probably regret it."

There were times in the next few weeks I didn't think either of us would live long enough to regret anything.

As soon as Hannah washed up after our noon meal she left and Oma and I began. The therapist had given Oma ten exercises. Oma insisted on increasing the number of times she did each one every day. Beads of sweat would pop up on her forehead and drop off her chin. Sometimes her face went as white as the sheets on her bed. But she kept on lifting and stretching her sorry leg.

I pulled, pushed, massaged, and grunted right along with her. Half of the time I was scared to death someone would find out what we were doing. The other half I wished someone would.

When the shoes came Oma tore into the package like a kid on Christmas morning. She jerked the shoes out of the box and started laughing. "These are the ugliest things I ever saw!"

"Who cares? Try them on."

We laced the shoes and Oma stood, holding on to the back of her wheelchair. Now both feet touched the floor.

"Oh, my, that feels good. Here, take this." She shoved the chair away.

The leg held her for a few seconds, then buckled. Oma fell backward onto the bed. She was laughing!

I was having a heart attack.

"I stood on my own two feet, Margo. Isn't that wonderful?"

All I could do was nod.

Oma sat up. "Back to work. Seems as if I have a ways to go before I walk."

I just couldn't say no to my gutsy grandmother.

All of Oma's conditioning took place between one o'clock and three. My conditioning went on all day.

The first time I walked to town and back it took me three hours. I collected six books from the library and the same number of blisters on my feet.

We worked out a nutritious, low calorie diet plan. Oma soon knew the number of calories in everything from asparagus to zucchini.

I didn't have to know calories. All I had to remember was that if I liked it I could have only a small portion. No second or third helpings. The first week of my diet was murder. True torture is picking cherries all morning for a pie you can have only a taste of!

Picking cherries and walking weren't my only exercise. Oma was good at inventing things which

11

required physical activity. I worked in the vegetable garden, went on errands to neighbors' houses (two miles, at least) and exercised the two horses Opa kept around for us grandchildren. And I was surprised, too—a lot of it was fun.

Progress was slow but eventually we could see some results. Oma's sorry leg filled out and got firmer. I began to shrink and get firmer.

Our plan was going well until Hannah became suspicious of my eating habits. The less I ate the more she speculated.

"Could be a tapeworm. I heard about a girl over in Montgomery County had a tapeworm. She started wasting away just like you."

"Did she die?" I asked with suitable horror.

"No. She lived . . . after they pulled a twenty foot worm out of her."

"That's a terrible story, Hannah," Oma scolded. "Margo doesn't have a tapeworm or any other disease. She's just trying to eat sensibly."

Hannah's loud snort let us know she wasn't fooled. Anyone who would turn down her strawberry shortcake for a bowl of plain berries (no cream, no sugar) was bound to be sick with something.

No amount of scolding from Oma could stop Hannah from tempting me with pies, cakes, and other fattening dishes.

"That's okay, Oma. Let her alone. It's good practice for when I get home. Mom's a lot like Hannah."

"Margaret's like Hannah? I don't believe it."

"Well, not exactly," I admitted, laughing. "Mom's a good cook though. And she's used to feeding Joel and Frank. They're football players, and with them big is better."

"Ah, I see. Well, your brothers are in for a little surprise, aren't they?"

"Everyone's in for a surprise," I said as Oma took four faltering steps all on her own.

Our surprise was almost discovered before we were ready. One day Opa came back to the house in the middle of the afternoon. We were in the bedroom. I'd just put on Oma's shoe and she was laughing about how clunky it looked.

"Is that you, Marta? Aren't you sleeping?" Opa called, coming down the hall.

Oma jumped into bed and under the covers, shoes and all. "I'm awake, Horst."

Opa came into the room, wiping his face with a blue bandanna. "Too hot for sleeping, eh? Maybe you'd be cooler on the porch?"

I wasn't sure whether to laugh or cry. I knew I must look as guilty as sin.

Oma looked guilty, too. "No . . . no, I should try to rest even if I can't sleep. Right, Margo?"

"Uh-hu—Yes, ma'am." I could see Opa looking at the big lumps under the covers. "Want a glass of lemonade, Opa? Come on, I'll fix it for you."

"I could use one," he answered, looking from me to Oma to the lumps.

I practically dragged him into the kitchen. I chattered like a bluejay, figuring if I kept talking he couldn't ask questions. I'm not a very good liar.

Opa didn't ask me anything at all. He drank his lemonade, thanked me, and went back to the fields. After that, he never came back to the house in the

13

middle of the afternoon. Sometimes at night though, I'd catch him watching us with a twinkle in his eyes. He knew we were up to something but he never said a word.

The night before my parents came to take me home Oma declared she was ready. "You go into the parlor and keep Opa company. I'll join you in a few minutes."

When she walked, tall and proud, into the room I thought I'd burst with happiness.

The look on Opa's face was a sight to behold. His "Glory be! Glory be!" sounded like a prayer.

"See, Horst? Dr. Baumgartner doesn't know everything," Oma said when he released her from a bear hug. "Margo and I know how to make secret wishes come true. Don't we, Margo?"

I was too choked up to speak so I just nodded.

Opa blew his nose and mumbled something into his handkerchief.

"What's that, Horst?"

"Spizerinktum," he replied, laughing. "Let's call the children."

"Let's wait and surprise them," Oma said. "Everyone will be here sometime tomorrow."

"All right, Dumpling. This is your show," Opa agreed.

They sat together on the sofa, holding hands. It made my throat ache just to watch them.

Everyone was very surprised when Oma walked out to greet them. She had to re-tell her story to each new wave of relatives. And she made my part sound much bigger than it really was. I protested but my aunts, uncles, cousins, and family refused to listen.

"You've worked a miracle," Aunt Lilo said. "Don't be modest."

"I didn't do anything except be here. Oma did this on her own."

"You certainly weren't indoors all of the time," Dad said. "You're as brown as a nut."

"And as skinny as a string bean," Mom added. "Have you been sick?"

I gave Oma an I-told-you-so look. "No, Mom. I'm as healthy as a horse."

"That's right, Margaret," Oma said. "Margo's been eating light and exercising. Doesn't she look wonderful?"

Mom smiled. "It takes a little getting used to but you do look very nice, Margo."

"It was time for her to lose her baby fat," Aunt Lilo said. "Lose a few more pounds, Margo, and you can compete for Miss Teenage America."

My brothers thought this was hilarious. So did I, for that matter. I put my hands on my hips and did a little hip-swinging strut. "How's this, Aunt Lilo?"

Everyone laughed—except Mom. "We don't approve of that kind of competition, Lilo. Margo doesn't need to be a fashion model to get ahead in life."

"Not to worry, Mom," I said quickly. "A Miss America I'm not."

I just wish Joel and Frank hadn't agreed so quickly.

Before we left Sunday morning Oma took me aside. "We've made my secret wish come true, Margo. I won't feel right until yours does."

15

"I'll have to wait until spring, Oma. That's when cheerleaders are selected."

"But you will try out?"

"At the very first chance. I promise."

"In the meantime you'll eat right and keep exercising?"

"Yes, ma'am. I may not be a Miss America but I won't be Miss Fat-n-Flab either."

Oma gave me a big hug. "You'll keep in touch?"

"I promise to write you every week."

"Now, Margo . . ."

"I don't make promises I don't intend to keep," I said. "You'll see."

Chapter 2

Day of Surprises

I wasn't the only thing that shrank over the summer. Ruffner looked much smaller when I walked in on Monday morning.

"Margo! Is that you?" Cindy squealed when she saw me. "Becca, look at Margo . . . what's left of her anyway."

Happiness poured over me like a warm shower. "I haven't lost that much. Besides, I grew an inch."

"Lucky you," Cindy muttered. Everything about Cindy is small except her heart.

"O-h-h! You look terrific," Becca said. "Won't you-know-who be surprised?"

Cindy rolled her eyes. "I'll say!"

"Who?" I asked, looking from one grinning face to the other.

"Guess."

"He's tall and really cute when he isn't moping around," hinted Becca.

"He sure had a long face when he found out you weren't coming to the party," added Cindy.

"WHO?" I demanded, going for Cindy's throat.

She dodged away. "Jeff. That's who."

I felt my face turning red. "Jeff Johnson?"

Cindy nodded. "You know, my neighbor. The boy you had a crush on all last year . . ."

"I know who Jeff is," I interrupted. "Are you sure he asked about me?"

"You're the only Margo I know," Becca said. "Must be you."

Another friend, Andrea Gibson, joined our group. Her enthusiasm over my new look helped cover my confusion. Of course they wanted to hear the details of my miracle weight loss. So I explained again how Oma and I had helped each other. They loved Oma, Opa, and, especially, Hannah.

A group of seventh graders scurried past us like frightened mice. "Did we look that lost and scared last year?" Andrea asked.

"I probably looked and felt worse," I replied. Even remembering caused a small knot in my stomach.

"I don't know how I looked but I sure was lost," Cindy said.

"You got lost? You're kidding!"

"No joke. I got turned around when I got off the bus and couldn't find the auditorium."

"I remember. You came into assembly late and sat beside me," I said. "You didn't look scared. You looked steamed."

"I was. I found the cafeteria . . . the gym . . . and the boys' locker room before I discovered the auditorium."

"What did it look like?" Becca demanded.

"What did what look like?"

18

"The boys' locker room!"

"Was anyone in there?" asked Andrea. Cindy pretended to zip her lips. "I'll never tell."

"Ve haf vays to make you talk," Andrea said, advancing on Cindy. "Right, comrades?"

Cindy was saved by the bell. Before we scattered to our homerooms, she gave me a nudge. "This is a great surprise, Margo. I'm proud of you. I bet it wasn't easy."

"I liked your surprise, too," I said, blushing as I thought of Jeff.

It felt so good to have friends, to have a place at Ruffner. And, though I'd never tell anyone, it felt great to be back in school. I like learning. I like the smell of books and chalk. I like teachers and challenges. I'm an oddball, I guess.

After Mrs. Bolton called the roll she made a surprising announcement. "Class, when the next bell rings you are to go to the auditorium instead of your scheduled class. Mr. Zale has some important news for us."

I looked across the aisle at Becca. She gave an I-don't-know shrug. When the bell rang she grabbed my hand and said, "Let's go save some good seats."

"Anybody know what's up?" Cindy asked when she found us.

Nobody around us had a clue.

Becca stood up and looked over the audience. "Has anyone seen Brandy yet?"

"No! Thank goodness," Cindy said.

"Why would you want to see her?" Andrea asked.

"Because I heard she spent the summer in France. I want to see the fabulous clothes she'll be wearing."

"Maybe she stayed in France," Cindy said hopefully. Brandy liked to pick on me but Cindy was her number one rival for every honor at school.

"No such luck. The Wines came back last week. I know because my brothers took care of their lawn this summer."

Our principal, assistant principal, and an absolutely smashing blond woman filed onto the stage.

"Wow! Who's she?" Cindy said.

Mr. Zale came to the microphone and made a welcoming speech. He captured our full attention when he said, "This is the last year two-thirds of you will be in this school." He paused to let his words sink in. "The new high school facility will be completed by next fall—six months ahead of schedule. Our present eighth and ninth grade students will be the freshman and sophomores in the new four-year high school. Ruffner Middle School will then be composed of the sixth, seventh and eighth grades. In other words, our present seventh graders will be our seniors next year."

A scraggly cheer rose from the seventh grade section.

"That's not fair," Cindy hissed.

"Why?"

"Because we'll be at the bottom again before we ever reach the top!"

The ninth graders do get extra privileges. I hadn't thought of that.

Evidently, Mr. Zale had thought of the same thing. "We know our eighth graders will miss out on being

20

seniors, so we've made some changes this year. Our assistant principal, Mr. Ortego, will tell you about the academic program."

"I thought you said there wouldn't be any surprises this year," I whispered to Cindy while Mr. Ortego explained the new courses to be offered.

"You know I'm lousy at predictions," she retorted.

"Sh-h-h!" Helen warned. "They're coming to the important part."

Finally, Mr. Zale introduced the beautiful blond woman. Miss Patricia Cole was going to tell us the changes in our extra-curricular activities.

Miss Cole was totally awesome. Everything about her sparkled—her deep blue eyes, her bouncy curls, her white teeth, her wide smile.

"Good morning, students. Besides being a physical education instructor, I am your new cheerleading coach. This year our squad will be increased from six to ten members. You now have four ninth graders and two eighth. We will add two more from eighth grade and two from the seventh. All students interested in trying out for these four slots may sign up at the physical education office. Practice sessions will begin tomorrow, with tryouts in two weeks . . ."

I have no idea what else she said. All I could hear was my promise to Oma, "I'll try out at the first chance." And my boast, "I don't make promises I can't keep." I wasn't ready! This wasn't supposed to happen till spring.

A few minutes later Cindy nudged me to my feet. "Get a move on, Margo. We have to sign up."

"I don't have to!"

21

"I thought you wanted to take computer science."

"Oh . . . oh, yes, I do."

"What's wrong?"

"Nothing."

"Nothing? You look zapped."

"I'm okay." I lied. My stomach was churning butterflies.

Someone yelled, "Hey, Cindy, you gonna try out for cheerleader?"

"No way!"

"How about you, Becca?" Andrea asked. "You're good in gymnastics."

"No way. I have dance, piano, *and* gymnastics this year. One more activity and I'll need to be twins."

No one bothered to ask me.

Brandy came sailing down the hall on a sea of expensive perfume, her fan club in tow. "Hi, guys!" she trilled.

"Hi, Brandy," Becca responded flatly. "How was your summer in Europe?"

"All right—if you care for old castles, palaces, and churches. Personally, I'm glad to be stateside again. Cindy, you're going out for cheerleader, aren't you?"

"Nope."

"But you're so athletic! You go to all the games. You should do it for our school."

"Ruffner will survive without me. Like you said last year, Brandy, cheerleading means working and sweating. I'll bet you aren't trying out."

"Of course she is! We talked her into it," Elicia Howard, Brandy's number one fan, said.

"Good luck," Cindy said and walked away.

"Well! I certainly expected more school spirit from Cindy," Brandy said. "I'm really disappointed."

The fan club nodded, copying Brandy's sad expression.

We went back to our homerooms to fill out new class schedules. Then we followed the old ones until our parents could approve of the changes. No one was doing much teaching or learning today.

It was a good thing nothing important was taught. All I could think about was cheerleading. Did my promise count in this new situation? If I did try out, would my friends think I was stupid? What if I did try out and I made a fool of myself? Did I really want to be a cheerleader? The only question I could answer was the last one. I did want to be a cheerleader.

Cheerleading and the new classes were the only topics of conversation at lunch. I nibbled my carrot sticks and kept quiet.

"What's eating you?"

"Carrot sticks."

Andrea's laugh rang through the cafeteria. "I asked what's eating you. Not what you're eating."

"Sorry. I was thinking about something."

"Must be pretty heavy-duty. Anything I can do to help?"

I shook my head. "No. Thanks for the offer but this is something I have to work out myself." Picking up my tray, I left my friends speculating on who our new spirit leaders would be—Carol, Brandy, Jill, Debbie, Helen, Sue . . .

By the time school let out I'd made a decision— sort of. It wouldn't do any harm to sign up. I could

23

always change my mind. Or I could say my parents wouldn't allow me. They might not. They might feel cheerleading tryouts were like Miss America contests.

I hung around school until there weren't any other girls in the PE office. Miss Cole was sitting at a desk. "I'd like to sign up, please."

"Join the crowd," she said, pointing to a clipboard.

At least she didn't laugh. The first page was already full of names. I signed at the bottom of the second sheet.

Miss Cole handed me a stack of papers. "These forms must be filled out and signed by your parents before you begin. Except for the physical examination sheet. You have until next Monday to get that done. The blue book is a book of game rules and referees' signals. You have to pass a written test on that material. Understood?"

I think I answered, "Yes, ma'am." My heart was beating so loudly it made my ears ring.

I'd missed my bus but I didn't care. I needed time to think as well as the exercise.

Chapter 3

Ready! Begin!

"May I call Oma to see how she's doing?" I asked after dinner.

"Go ahead, Dumpling," Dad said. "That's very thoughtful of you."

I felt a twinge of guilt for lying about my reason. "Thanks, Dad." I ran upstairs so I could talk privately.

"Tell Oma we asked about her," Mom requested.

"I will."

After Opa and I exchanged family news Oma got on the line.

"Hi. Opa said you went to the doctor. What did he say?"

Oma chuckled. "Dr. Baumgartner said now he'd seen two miracles."

"Two?"

"The first was an old lady like me walking. The second was how I did it in mail-order shoes. He sent me lickety-split to an orthopedic specialist for shoes. My new footwear should be here in a week or so.

He—Dr. James—promised they'd feel and look much better."

"Good. How's Hannah taking this?"

"Like you'd expect. She knows a woman in my exact-same situation who fell and broke her other leg. Now this woman's a permanent cripple."

"Poor Hannah. She sure knows a lot of unfortunate people, doesn't she?"

"I'll say! I just wish I didn't have to meet all of them. How's your fitness program coming along?"

I explained my new predicament. "I know I promised to take the first opportunity but that was when I thought I had a whole school year to get ready. What should I do?"

"You could wait until spring," Oma said, letting me off the hook.

"I wouldn't stand a chance of making the high school squad without experience."

"So if you're going to be a cheerleader it's now or never?"

"That's about it. . . . But I'm afraid, Oma."

"Of what?"

"Looking stupid. None of my friends expect me to try out. They named half of the girls at Ruffner but not me."

"You ever mention how much you want to be a cheerleader?"

"No."

"Any mind readers in your group?"

"No," I said, laughing.

Oma was serious. "Then maybe you're not being fair to your friends. What others expect doesn't amount to a hill of beans anyway, Margo. It's what you expect from yourself that counts. So what if you don't make the team? Nobody succeeds at everything they try. But nobody succeeds at anything *unless* they try."

I suddenly remembered Oma's pale face, dripping sweat, as she struggled to make her sorry leg work again. "You're right, Oma. Thanks."

While I still had the courage I gathered the forms and went back downstairs.

"How is Mama?" Dad asked, looking up from his paper.

"She's fine and she sends her love. Can I talk to you and Mom for a minute?"

Dad put down his paper and Mom closed her book.

"I want to be a cheerleader."

"A cheerleader? When did you get this notion?" Mom asked.

"I've always wanted to be one. Today I got the courage and a chance. We have a new coach, Miss Cole. She wants two more eighth grade cheerleaders and two from seventh. I'd like to try out."

"I don't see any reason you shouldn't," Dad said.

"It's very expensive," I cautioned. "I'll have to have new shorts, shoes, socks and stuff, plus a physical exam. Also you have to agree to chaperone and provide some transportation. I mean, if I make it."

"We've been through this before with sandlot and Little League," Mom said. "I'm sure we could manage to do this for you."

"Let's see those forms," Dad requested.

I couldn't believe it was so easy. I gave them the papers and waited while they read them.

27

"Miss Cole certainly spells things out very clearly," Dad said, reaching for his pen. "She's running the cheering squad just like any other sport."

"I approve of the code of conduct and her emphasis on maintaining your grades," Mom said.

Dad thumbed through the rule book. "I'll bet there aren't many girls who know as much about as many different sports as you do, Margo."

"Thanks to Joel and Frank. However, that's not the part I'm worried about passing."

"You'll do just fine, Dumpling."

"I'll call Dr. Jaggers about a physical. You were due for one anyway. Would Saturday morning be all right?" Mom asked.

"That's the *only* time. We have practice every day after school."

It didn't take long to get my gym stuff together. Getting to sleep was a different matter. Instead of counting sheep I went through every cheer I ever knew, even making up a few new ones.

When morning came I showered, dressed, and made my bed like someone swimming underwater.

"Hurry up, Margo. You'll miss your bus," Mom called.

"I'm coming."

I knew the reason I was dragging my feet. My brothers! Mom had probably told them about my venture. If they teased me I knew I'd cry. And my tears come easily. The old Wagner Waterworks. Today they were gathered at the edge of my eyes just waiting to stage a cloudburst.

Fortunately, Joel and Frank had finished breakfast and were going out the door when I came down. Frank whizzed past me with a "Good luck, Margo."

Joel stopped. "Cheerleading's hard, physical work, Margo. Are you sure you want to spend the time and energy?"

"Why shouldn't I?"

Joel backed off. "Hey, just so you're sure."

"I'm sure!"

"Then go for it, Sis."

Mom made me eat breakfast. "You need a good foundation. I packed some raisins in your lunch, too."

"Will you pick me up at five?"

"I'll be waiting in the parking lot just as you asked," Mom assured me. "Now, scoot!"

When I got of the bus I was surprised to see Brandy hanging around where the buses drop us off. I knew she didn't ride a bus. Her folks brought her to school every day. She must have been waiting for someone. I said, "Hi," and started inside.

Brandy fell into step beside me. "How was your summer, Margo? You look terrific!"

"Just fine, thanks. How was yours? I heard you went to Europe."

"I did. It was just fab! We were in France for a whole month. I learned to speak French," Brandy said, preening.

"Neat! Was it hard?"

"Not really. My tutor said I have an ear for languages. Margo, I have a favor to ask."

"What?"

"It's not really for me. It's for the school. Cindy would make such a good cheerleader. You're her

29

best friend. Won't you *please* talk her into trying out?"

I was speechless. Since when had Brandy been so concerned about Ruffner?

"I know you're surprised," Brandy said, reading my reaction correctly. "We were so childish last year. I'm sure we've grown up over the summer. We want Ruffner to be the best school in the district, don't we? Will you talk to her?"

Brandy looked so sincere. People *do* change. I nodded. "Okay. I'll try."

Brandy gave my arm a friendly squeeze. "I knew I could count on you, Margo. You're *ma trés belle amie!*"

Leaving me trying to figure out that one, she waltzed off to join her friends. I went to my locker in a daze.

"What was Brandy being so chummy about?" Andrea asked.

"She learned to speak French this summer," I answered absently. I just couldn't figure out any advantage for Brandy in this.

"Oh, goody! Now she can be nasty in two languages."

"Actually, she was very nice. Maybe she's changed."

My statement drew mixed reactions. A thoughtful nod from Becca and a rude noise from Andrea.

"A summer in Europe can't change that girl," Andrea said. "Brandy was born mean."

"I don't think so," Becca said. "I don't think Brandy—or anybody—is born mean. There isn't a gene for mean. My father said so. He said people aren't born bad. It's something they learn."

Andrea didn't look convinced. "So Brandy's a fast learner. You be careful, Margo."

"Where's Cindy?" I asked, remembering my promise.

"She went to put her sax in the band room." Becca answered. "Are you going to take any of the new classes, Margo?"

"Computer science is all I have room for."

"Oh-ho! We know why you're taking that class, don't we, guys?" Becca said.

"Yeah. His initials are J.J.," Andrea said.

I felt myself blushing. "That's *not* the reason!"

The bell saved me from more teasing. I was upset in more ways than one. Now I'd have to wait until lunch to talk to Cindy. I wanted her to be the first to know that I was trying out and try to get her to join me.

It was no go. Cindy as adamant. She wasn't one bit interested in being on the squad. She was, however, very supportive of me.

"Hey, gang! Guess who else is trying out?" she sang out to our table at lunch. "Margo! Isn't that great? Now we have two to cheer for every day."

"Who besides me?" I asked.

"Me," Helen said with a grin. "Remember, I tried out last spring. I've always wanted to be a cheerleader."

To tell the truth, I'd forgotten about Helen Bronoski and how upset she'd been last spring when she didn't make it. "Well, you're one up on me. At least you'll know the ropes, Helen."

"We'll come every day and cheer you on," Cindy said.

31

"Practices are closed this year," Helen said. "You can come to the tryouts though."

It really gave me a boost when no one laughed about me wanting to be a cheerleader. I was still feeling pretty up when I turned in my forms at the beginning of PE class. I got another boost from Miss Fitz.

During our volleyball match she said, "Nice serve, Margo! You're looking good."

I knew she was talking about volleyball but it made me feel wonderful anyway.

I had showered and was dressing when my new pen fell out of my notebook and rolled under the lockers. I was down on my hands and knees searching for it when I overheard something that made me feel awful.

"Is Cindy Cunningham's name on the list yet?" Elicia's voice asked.

"I don't think so. Why?"

"If I tell you, promise you won't tell?"

"Cross my heart."

"It's a set up. Cindy will sign up. Brandy has Margo working on her. Cindy will try out and this time Brandy will cream her!"

"How can you be sure?"

"Because Brandy didn't spend the *whole* summer in Europe. She attended the National Cheerleading Camp so she'd be ready for high school tryouts next year. She's a sure thing, believe me."

Elicia and the other girl moved away. I got up from my cramped position feeling lower than a worm. Andrea was right. Brandy hadn't changed. She was out for revenge. And, worse, she was using me. I was just too dumb to know it. I was so ashamed of myself I didn't even tell anybody what I'd heard.

I was still feeling pretty low when I went into the gym after school. What I saw didn't make me feel any better. A huge crowd of girls was milling nervously around the gym. You didn't need to be good at math to figure the odds—especially if the deck was stacked in one person's favor.

I found Helen and was about to tell her about Brandy when a shrill whistle brought all conversation to a halt. All eyes turned in the direction of the whistle.

Miss Cole came flying onto the gym floor in a series of cartwheels and back flips. She finished by landing in a perfect split, yelling, "Go, Ruffner!"

We cheered.

She quieted us with another blast of her whistle. "Girls, that's just a small sample of what our squad will be doing by the end of the year. We are going to have the best cheerleaders in the whole district! Right?"

"Right!" we shouted.

"Good! Now . . . only four of you will be added to the squad. I expect the rest of you to be in the stands supporting your teams and your cheerleaders. Will you do that?"

"Yes!"

"That's the spirit! Line up in a straight line. Now, count off in groups of five. Good. This is your squad. These are the five girls you'll practice with every day. Circle the squads. Count off, squads."

I was in squad four with Helen and three seventh graders I didn't know.

"First rule: *Always* warm up and stretch out before you begin cheering," Miss Cole said. "Squads one through four, line up over here. Five through eight, over there. Leave plenty of room between squads and each other."

We spread out over the whole gym.

Miss Cole stood in the middle and demonstrated some exercises. "Now, follow me. Ready! Begin!'

For twenty-five minutes we jogged, did leg lifts, arm circles, toe curls, leg kicks, and side twists. I was breathless when Miss C. finally whistled us to a halt.

"That . . . wasn't so bad," Helen panted.

"Yeah . . . I always . . . said oxygen . . . was over-rated."

"If this had been tryouts all of you would have failed!" Miss Cole announced. "Do you know why? You weren't smiling. Rule two: A cheerleader *always* smiles."

"Oh, sure!" muttered the girl beside me. Sweat was running off her chin and dripping onto her T-shirt.

I grinned—or tried to.

"Circle your squads. Each squad will have a cheerleader to work with you—either one of our own or one of the high school squad. Begin by introducing yourselves. Today we will work on the basic hand, arm, and foot positions. And remember—SMILE!"

Helen and I introduced ourselves to Janet, Gina, and Freddi, the seventh graders. Our leader was Mitzi Learner. She's co-captain of the Ruffner squad.

Although I've been watching cheerleaders for years, I never realized there were so many different things to learn. Every part of your body is important. Fingers, fists, arms, and wrists must be held the proper way. Not to mention feet forward, knees bent, hips under, tummy in, chest high, lips in a permanent smile. All of this and we hadn't learned one yell.

After Mitzi finished with us we had to do twenty-five more minutes of conditioning exercises.

My butt was dragging when I hobbled out to the car. I had a smile on my face though.

So did thirty-nine other girls. We must have looked pretty weird as we limped out of the gym, hot, tired, and sweaty, but still smiling.

"How was it?" Mom asked.

"Won-der-ful," I said, trying to get my upper lip to slide over my dry teeth.

"Everyone's smiling."

"Of course."

Chapter 4

No Pain, No Gain

I was not smiling when I woke up the next morning. Every movement sent waves of pain over my whole body.

Very slowly, I tried to sit up. Great agony. I fell back. What was I supposed to do? What if I had damaged myself permanently? Was anything worth this pain? What if I were doomed to spend the rest of my life flat on my back in this bed?

Just before my waterworks turned on full blast, I heard Joel's heavy tread in the hall. "Jo-el," I croaked. "Joel, help me."

"Margo?"

"Joel, come in here, please."

"What's up?"

"I can't move. I think I've broken my whole body."

"Sore, huh?"

"That doesn't begin to describe how I feel! What am I going to do?"

"Get up and take a shower. It'll help."

"I can't move. It hurts."

36

Sometimes Joel can be an insensitive clod. Without warning, he grabbed my arm and hauled me to my feet.

"There! You're up. Hit the showers, Sis."

"My legs won't move."

With a sigh, Joel put his arm around my waist and pulled me toward the bathroom. "Want me to give you a bath? Or can you manage?"

"I can manage, thank you."

Joel patted my head. "No pain, no gain, Sis!"

"Don't! Even my hair hurts."

The hot shower helped. I managed—with grunts and groans—to get dressed.

Joel helped me downstairs. "You'd better not let Mom see that pain on your face," he warned. "You know how she gets."

With an effort, I straightened up and walked into the kitchen with a big smile on my face. My performance was worthy of an Oscar.

When I got to school I noted all the other cheerleading hopefuls were stumbling around as painfully as I was. All, that is, except Brandy. She skipped around the halls full of smiles and good cheer.

"You'll feel fine in an few days," she told me.

"Aren't you just a little bit sore?"

"No. But then I just came back from cheerleading camp last week."

I had a surprising urge to kick her shins so she'd have at least one ache. "I heard you'd been to camp," I said through clenched teeth. "And I'm glad your sneaky plan didn't work."

"What plan?" Brandy asked, all wide-eyed and innocent.

"You wanted Cindy to try out just so you could beat her at something."

"No, I just wanted some decent competition. Beating a bunch of marshmallows isn't any fun. Besides, you can't prove a thing!"

She was right. I couldn't prove anything. Brandy hadn't broken any rules. There's nothing wrong with encouraging competition. Besides, I had other worries. Like how was I going to get through the day? I wasn't looking forward to the practice session either. *If* I made it that far.

Miss Cole did not look happy when she came into the gym. "I don't think we have any cheerleaders in this crowd! All day long I've seen nothing but long, sour faces in the halls. A cheerleader *always* smiles. It doesn't matter how she *feels*. A cheerleader S-M-I-L-E-S! Can you remember that?"

"Yes, ma'am," we answered raggedly.

"I can't hear you!"

"YES, MA'AM!"

"I don't see those smiles."

Everyone smiled until it hurt.

"That's better. Keep those teeth showing. People will be watching you and reporting to me. Now, line up for stretches."

For twenty minutes we jumped, jogged, and beat our sore bodies to Miss Cole's merciless count. With big smiles on our faces, too.

When she finally took pity on us and said, "Take five," we collapsed where we stood.

After my lungs got enough air into them I said to

38

Helen, "You know that old expression 'I died laughing'? Well, it just might come true in my case."

"Dying sounds good," Helen said. "I think she's trying to kill us off. She may be the first PE teacher tried for mass murder."

"Sh-h! She might hear you," Janet hissed, looking scared.

Maybe Miss C. did hear us. Whispers carry in the gym. All I know is that we hadn't seen anything yet. With a wicked gleam in her eye, Miss C. had us form our squads and began teaching us a few simple jumps.

Simple? Miss C. and the cheerleaders demonstrated fourteen different jumps. None of them was simple.

"You will be required to do two jumps at tryouts," Miss Cole announced. "A C jump and one other jump of your choice. Remember, you always jump *facing* the crowd. Now, squads, practice your C jump."

"Okay, listen up," Mitzi said to our squad. "This is your basic jump technique. Take one step forward, swing both arms down, bring your feet together. Lift with your arms, head and chest, look forward, not down. Point your toes, extend your legs, jump up, and tuck your legs back. Land on the balls of your feet with your knees bent. Like this."

Mitzi demonstrated and we tried to imitate her. Miss Cole roved from squad to squad checking our progress.

When Miss C. ended practice she had some final words of advice. "Tomorrow we'll learn our cheer. Then you'll have everything you need for tryouts. Success is achieved by practice, practice, practice, and more practice. Over the weekend I want you to cheer for your mother, your father, your neighbors, your dog, and your mirror! Next week you'll work with your squads on timing and voice. Cheerleading is a team effort; therefore, you will help each other become better. We only want the best for Ruffner. Right, girls?"

"Right!"

Miss C. seemed satisfied and dismissed us.

Helen and I collected our books from the bleachers.

"I don't know why I bother taking these books home," she complained. "I'm too pooped to study. All I want to do is eat and fall in bed."

"I'll even skip the eating," I said. "I guess we're lucky most of the teachers haven't assigned any homework."

Janet overheard us. Her eyes filled with tears. "I'm not lucky. All of my teachers have. They're all dragons!"

I remembered how scared I'd been last year. "They're not so bad, Janet. They just want you to get started on the right foot."

"I'm not worried about most of them," Janet admitted, sniffing. "But Miss Kilper scares me to death. I'm not very good in math."

"You will be after Old Killer gets through with you," Helen retorted. "You'll learn math if it kills you."

"Don't worry about it," I said quickly. "She's a good teacher. Give her a chance."

"Sure," Janet said. But she didn't look convinced as she limped away clutching her math book.

"You weren't much help!" I scolded Helen. "You scared the wits out of Janet."

40

"I told the truth," Helen snapped. Without even saying goodbye, she got in her mother's car and they drove away.

I had to wait a few minutes for Mom.

"Sorry I'm late," she said when I collapsed in the front seat.

"That's okay. I'm sorry to put you through this. It will only be for two weeks."

After today I didn't have much hope of being selected as a cheerleader. So why was I willing to go through this pain?

Chapter 5

Practice, Practice, Practice

"If I hear that yell one more time I'll croak!"

"Don't you know any others?"

"Yeah, a little variety would help."

My brothers were picking on me after my weekend of practice. The floodgates of Wagner Waterworks— of which I am President and Chairman of the Board—threatened to open. "I told you it's the cheer we have to do at tryouts!"

"Have a little patience, boys," Dad said. "Practice makes perfect—as I'm sure you know since you're in sports."

I gave Dad a watery smile and tightened the taps on my tears. "It will all be over on Friday. Can you guys hold out till then?"

With Mom and Dad glaring across the dinner table at them, my brothers nodded.

I was as sick of the stupid yell as they were. All weekend Helen and I had practiced together. We even gave up going skating with our friends. And here it was Sunday night and I hadn't done my homework. I was hoarse and sore and tired. I sure wasn't in any mood for their teasing or complaining.

Later, when Mom came upstairs to make me turn out my light, she said, "Margo, are you sure this is what you want?"

"You mean being a cheerleader? Sure, Mom. I want it more than anything. Why?"

"Well, you sounded so sad when you told Cindy you couldn't go to the skating rink. And you're always so tired! You live, eat, and breathe cheerleading."

"This is the hard part, Mom. If I don't make the squad, then on Friday I'll go back to being just plain old Margo. If I should, by some miracle, make it I'm sure it won't take up so much of my time."

"I certainly hope so! Being a cheerleader isn't nearly as important as your health. Now, turn out your light and get some sleep, Dumpling."

I grinned. "Okay, Mom. Just let me finish these two problems."

The first thing I noticed at Monday's practice session was our dwindling numbers. We'd lost eight girls over the weekend. Freddi had dropped from our squad.

"She sprained her ankle Saturday," Janet explained. "The doctor said she couldn't jump on it for six weeks."

Freddi was the least co-ordinated member of our group. She had no sense of rhythm. She was always half a beat behind the rest of us. I was sorry she'd hurt herself but glad she wouldn't be embarrassed at tryouts.

43

"This is just the beginning," Mitzi warned us. "By Friday we'll be down to twenty-five girls."

"How do you know?" demanded Helen.

"From experience. Mine and my sister's. Carey's a cheerleader at the high school. She says it's always this way. The real losers always drop out first."

"That's not fair! Freddi couldn't help hurting her ankle," I said.

Mitzi gave me a hard look. "Very convenient timing, wasn't it?"

Gina giggled. "Freddi was pretty awful."

"Maybe ... it's ... for ... the best," Helen huffed, jogging in place.

"You're going to hear some far-out excuses before this is over," Mitzi said. "Just wait and see. Maybe they ought to give an award for the funniest excuse."

"Keep a list," Helen said spitefully.

Everyone giggled.

I thought they were being mean.

Mitzi was right though. Each day a few more girls dropped out. There were lots of reasons: injuries, allergies, doctor's orders, mean parents, and other pressing responsibilities. It was never the fault of any girl that she couldn't compete.

I laughed along with everyone else as each new excuse made the rounds. But, somehow, it made me sad. The girls who dropped out were labeled losers by every girl in the middle school gym. And in middle school, labels stick! I wondered if those who didn't make the squad would be labeled the same way. I asked Mitzi.

"Of course not!" she replied. "At least the girls who finish have guts!"

That was some small comfort. Enough to keep me jumping, clapping, and yelling through one more practice. At least I wasn't quite so sore.

Cindy called me for the usual progress report right after dinner. "Hi! It's me. How did it go today?"

"Just great. I made wonderful baskets, candlesticks, and buckets."

"What?"

"Oh, those are the easy things . . . just what to do with your hands. Hands I know. It's what to do with the rest of my body that's a problem."

"Like what?"

"Like a stag jump. I look more like a hippopotamus than a deer!"

"How does the rest of the squad look doing this stag jump?"

"About as graceful as I do," I replied, laughing.

"Aha! Just as I thought. Is it one of the harder jumps?"

"No, it isn't. A Herkie is much, much harder. I'll never learn that one. And, would you believe, Miss C. says we're going to learn to do cartwheels and back flips?"

"Not for tryouts!"

"No, but the new squad will. Miss C. says they're very impressive. She should know. She was a member of last year's National Championship college squad. Heck, Cindy, I get dizzy turning a somersault."

"Helen says you're good. She thinks you're going to make the squad."

"Really? Helen said that?"

"She sure did. Don't be discouraged, Margo."

"Well, it *is* good exercise," I admitted. "I don't

45

have to count calories anymore. Mostly, I'm too tired to eat."

My spirits soared and fell like a butterfly in a high wind. Every other day I felt like quitting. Most of my panic came from watching the other girls. They always looked much better than I felt.

One night when Cindy called I was really down. "What's wrong? Rough practice?"

"Cindy, I'm so tired I can sleep sitting up. I know that for a fact because I did it in science class. Mrs. Silvers turned on the lights after the movie and had to call my name three times before I woke up!"

"I always sleep through those movies. They're pretty awful. Not to worry."

"Well, I am worried about my English paper. It's due tomorrow and I haven't even begun. And to make matters worse, Mitzi picked on me all during practice."

"Why?"

"Who knows? All I know is that my voice didn't suit her. My enthusiasm was lacking. And my punches weren't crisp. By the end of practice I felt like punching her! Crisply, of course."

Cindy had a fit of giggles.

"What's so funny?"

"The idea of you punching anyone. You really must have been upset."

"Upset is good word," I said wryly. "When Miss C. came over to monitor our progress I fell flat on my fanny."

"What happened?"

"I didn't cry, if that's what you're asking. I picked myself up and finished the yell."

46

"Good for you! How's our friend Brandy doing?"

"She's good. In fact, Brandy's better than some of the cheerleaders. She deserves a place on the squad."

"Well, the gang is coming to tryouts and we're pulling for you and Helen."

"Thanks, Cindy. Now I have to go write this paper before I fail English. My grades aren't so hot so far."

"The worst is over," consoled Cindy. "After Friday things will settle down and you'll be a cheerleader and an *A* student again. Don't cave in now, Margo."

"Me? Old marshmallow Margo?"

"Who said you were a marshmallow?" demanded Cindy.

"Brandy. She said that's what her competition is—a bunch of marshmallows. But I don't think she knows much about us marshmallows. You can punch us but we bounce back."

The last day of practice was awful. On my solo run my timing was off and my voice cracked.

"Last day jitters," Mitzi assured me, smiling.

Helen was letter perfect, except for her thin, reedy voice. Janet and Gina were only fair.

While were were taking a short break I saw the strangest sight. Brandy was actually coaching another member of her squad. I poked Helen. "Look at that!"

"I don't believe it!"

Brandy was off to one side, working with a girl on her jumps. Step by step, she talked the girl through it. "Good! Try it again now. This time keep those toes pointed . . . all right! Perfect!"

Brandy's unselfishness wasn't going unnoticed. I saw Miss Cole smiling and pointing to the hard-working duo.

"That's really nice of Brandy," I said.

"Oh, sure," Helen drawled. "She doesn't have anything to fear from a seventh grader."

"She could be using the time to practice herself."

"She doesn't need the practice," Helen said. "She's earning Brownie points. Honestly, Margo, sometimes you're too nice for your own good!"

"I am not!"

"Are, too. You always believe the best about everyone."

"What's wrong with that?"

"Nothing. Unless you get burned," Helen said, shaking her head.

Miss Cole blew her whistle just then so we didn't get to finish our conversation.

"Girls, tomorrow is the big day. All of you have worked very hard. You are to be commended for sticking till the end . . . without any drastic injuries or silly excuses."

Her slight emphasis on 'drastic' and 'silly' caused a ripple of laughter.

After the laughter died away, Miss Cole continued, "Our first home soccer game is tonight. I expect to see all of you there supporting your team and your cheerleaders. Get a good night's sleep. Good luck tomorrow."

I obeyed one instruction. I went to the game. And, like the rest of the hopefuls, I made sure Miss C. saw me. I didn't enjoy the game very much. I was too busy watching the cheerleaders to watch the game.

"You'd better enjoy this," Cindy said around a mouthful of hot dog. "You won't be sitting in the stands with us anymore."

"Don't be so sure of that. I'll probably be sitting right here next week."

"I wouldn't mind," Jeff mumbled. He blushed and added quickly, "It's the only time you get to be with us."

"At least I get to see you in our computer class," I said smiling up at him.

"Here come the Ervine cheerleaders," Helen said. "Let's see how good or bad they are."

We happily dissected every move they made. Ruffner was definitely better.

As for Miss C.'s other order, I didn't or couldn't sleep very well. I dreamed of cheerleading all night. Someone shouted orders at me at a machine gun pace. "Side lunge! Punch! Smile! C jump! Chest high! Smile! Fingers together! Knees relaxed! Land on the balls of your feet. . . ."

Chapter 6

Tryouts

If wishing someone good luck helps then I had it made. By lunch time I'd been wished good luck a hundred times. Actually, it just made me more nervous. I couldn't forget, even for a minute, what was to take place at 3:10.

"Butterflies in your stomach, huh?" Cindy said sympathetically as I leaned against my locker before PE.

"Feels more like bullfrogs. I'd rather have butterflies. They're lighter."

"Can you tell how it's shaping up? I mean, who's good and who's not."

"Not really. We're too busy doing our own thing. But if yesterday is a sample, I don't have a prayer. I did everything wrong."

"My sister Ellen is into theater," Cindy said thoughtfully. "She says when the dress rehearsal is awful then opening night is a smash. Maybe this is the same way."

"I sure hope so. I'd hate to make a complete fool of myself."

"You won't! Remember we'll be there cheering for you."

If that was supposed to make me feel better, it didn't. I'd rather fail in front of strangers.

I wasn't nervous at all about the first part of our test which was given in our PE class. Following the guidelines of the National Cheerleaders Association, we were to be weighed, measured, and given a written exam on game rules and referees' signals. Our scores and measurements went right on the judges' scoring sheets.

Seven of the girls who were trying out were in my PE class. We lined up alphabetically to be weighed and measured. Brandy was right behind me as I stepped on the scales.

"Margo Wagner," Miss Cole called to the recorder. "One hundred-thirteen, five-four."

"Margo, that's wonderful!" Brandy exclaimed. "You've really lost weight. How many pounds have you lost?"

"About twenty since last fall," I replied, blushing with pleasure.

"Isn't that wonderful, Miss Cole? Doesn't she look great now?" Brandy said, clapping her hands.

Miss Cole nodded and called, "Next."

I smiled at Brandy. She really wasn't so bad. She was happy for me.

Helen thought differently. She was furious when we sat down to take the test. "Boy, what a rat-fink that Brandy is!"

"Why?"

Helen looked at me as if I had just landed on Planet Earth. "Are you dense, Hortense? There was

51

no need for Brandy to let Miss C. know that you were overweight last year!"

"But Brandy was complimenting me."

"Oh bro-ther! Don't you know if you gain weight they can kick you off the squad?" Helen said, rolling her eyes.

Miss Cole rapped on the desk for our attention. "Girls, as I've told you before, there is more to being a cheerleader than simply leading your classmates in cheers. You represent your school at all times. Therefore, you must always look good. But there's more to cheerleading than looking good and being popular. A good cheerleader must know *when* to cheer and which cheer is appropriate. After all, we don't want to yell 'We want a touchdown!' when our opponents are on the goal line, do we? Knowing your sports will help you decide on the proper cheer.

"This test, designed by the National Cheerleaders Association, will measure your knowledge of several sports. If you have studied the booklet I gave you, you will have no trouble with this test. Your score will count for twenty-five percent of your grade. Good luck."

I thought the test was easy. But Helen had a lot of trouble with the referees' signals. She hadn't attended the countless football, basketball, baseball, and soccer games that I had.

Tryouts were held in the gym. As soon as school let out all twenty-five of us gathered in the girls' locker room. Nothing smells quite like a room full of nervous girls spraying twenty-five brands of hair spray and deodorant. I could hardly breathe.

"Gather around, girls," Miss Cole said. "Your

judges will be Miss Fitz, Mrs. Ellis, the high school cheerleading coach, Elizabeth Cantrell, the captain of the high school squad, Mitzi, and myself. You are to enter the gym from here, do your cheer, then be seated with the audience. Position will be determined by drawing numbers from this hat. Line up and choose a number, please."

Brandy drew five.

Helen drew seven.

I drew seventeen.

"When you hear my whistle come out," Miss Cole said.

Jane Eastman, a seventh grader, was unlucky. She drew number one.

Fay Godwin, number three, fainted and had to be carried away. The delay took only ten minutes but it felt like hours.

One by one the girls began to move past me.

My mouth was dry. My body was damp. I needed to go to the bathroom—again. My head was spinning.

Did I really want to be a cheerleader? Yes! No matter how bad I felt at the moment, I really, really did.

The whistle sounded again. Number sixteen went out.

I blanked out everything—the room, the nervous girls, the pungent aromas—everything. I created a scene in my head. . . .

The night is crisp. The stands are full. We're playing for the district championship. Ruffner is on the twenty yard line. We are down by three points. Two minutes to go. Our guys need encouragement. Get the crowd into the game! It's up to you. . . .

Somewhere a whistle blew. Someone gave me a shove. I ran. The hardwood floor felt like turf. Get the crowd on their feet. . . . Let the team know we're with them. . . .

Hey, Hey! What do you say?
We've got the spirit!
We've got the might!
We've got the power
To win tonight!
Go, Ruffner! Score!

Loud applause brought me back to the gym. I'd done it! It was over. I smiled at the judges and took a seat.

"How did I do?" I whispered to Helen.

Helen gave me a funny look. "Better than you ever did in practice. Did you pop a pill or something?"

Helen didn't sound very friendly. It made me feel bad. I knew how much she wanted to be a cheerleader. After all, this was her second try.

"You were both terrific!" Cindy said when she and Becca came over.

"Helen, you defied the law of gravity on your jumps," Becca said. "You ought to be going out for gymnastics."

"Maybe I'll have to," Helen replied. "I don't think I made the squad."

"I didn't mean it like that!" Becca protested.

Helen shrugged and turned away. But not before I saw the hurt in her eyes.

The judges seemed to take forever. The gym echoed with shrill, nervous talking and laughter. The sounds grated on my ears. I wanted desperately for it to be over so I could go home.

Finally, Cindy cried, "Here comes Miss Cole!"

A deathly silence fell over the gym. I actually think my heart stopped for a beat or two.

"I want to thank all of you for your hard work. Unfortunately, we only have four slots to fill. Everyone can't have a place on the squad . . . this year. But Mrs. Ellis and I know we have some excellent material for next season. Now for the news you've been waiting for. Your new spirit leaders are . . . from the seventh grade, Lori Griffith and Patsy Burch. From the eighth grade, Brandy Wine and Margo Wagner. Congratulations!"

I was buried in an avalanche of hugs and good wishes.

"See? I told you so!" Cindy cried.

"Way to go, Margo!"

"Congratulations," Helen said, trying to hold her voice steady and keep back the tears.

"Thanks, Helen. I'm sorry you didn't make it." I said and meant it. My face was wet with tears. Some of them were for Helen and the others who didn't make the squad. Some were for me—marshmallow Margo—who'd toughed it out. Who made her secret wish come true. Victory was sweet.

I finally tore free of my well-wishers and went to change. The atmosphere in the locker room was very different now. Some girls fought to keep from crying. Others tried to act like they didn't care. Disappointment was thicker than the hair spray fumes.

Victory doesn't taste quite so sweet when it's

seasoned with other's tears. I felt so sorry for the twenty-one other girls.

"Why the long face, Margo? We won!" Brandy asked, sweeping into the room followed by her group of admirers.

My mouth fell open. How could she be so insensitive? At the sight of her gloating face the other girls practically slunk out of the room.

"Crowing isn't cool, Brandy," I said as soon as I found my voice.

"Just telling it like it is, Margo."

Miss Cole stuck her head into the room. "I'd like to see the new squad members in my office, please."

Lori, Patsy, Brandy, and I filed into the office. Three of us were still stunned by our good fortune.

Miss Cole was seated on top of her desk beside her big cheerleading trophy. "First, congratulations. You won your positions over a very good group. You were very good. *But* you are at a disadvantage. You didn't attend camp with squad. You haven't learned our cheers and you've never cheered before a crowd. We are going to overcome all of those disadvantages with hard work. Are you willing to do that?"

We all nodded.

"Good! We'll begin by having a practice session tomorrow. We need to get your uniforms from the extra ones we have on hand. They may need some mending and alterations but we'll make do.

"Now the other matter I need to discuss is your schedules. I have permission from Mr. Zale to make some schedule changes. I would like for the whole squad to have seventh period PE. That will give us a practice period every day. You will be excused from your regular PE classes but will get a grade from your cheerleading. Does anyone have any objection?"

There were several "no's."

I guess I was frowning because Miss Cole said, "Any problem, Margo?"

"Will we be able to take the same classes?"

"The same subjects but not in the same classes," Miss C. said, shuffling through some blue cards. "For example, Margo, you'll only change your algebra and computer science classes. It's so early in the year it shouldn't make any difference to you."

I had a brief pang of regret at not being in computer class with Jeff. "I guess it's okay."

"It doesn't make a bit of difference to me," Brandy said. "Anything for the squad."

Miss C. beamed. "That's the spirit, Brandy! There's no 'I' in team or squad. I want you girls to remember that. We are a team. A family. Sisters. We must do everything—big or small—to help one another become the best squad in the whole state. Do I have your pledge on that?"

"Yes!"

"Welcome to the squad!" Miss C. shouted.

The old squad members came running into the office yelling, "Welcome! Welcome!"

"Who are you?" Miss Cole asked, her voice rising effortlessly over the clamor.

"Ruffner Middle School!"

"What's our motto?"

"All for one and one for all!"

This was obviously a rehearsed act. But it was still pretty effective.

I left school floating on Cloud Twelve. Cloud Nine is for ordinary mortals.

Chapter 7

Another Wish Come True

Being a cheerleader really changed my life. Last year I walked down the halls without being noticed. This year everyone knows me. Last year I wasn't into anything except school work. This year I'm involved in practically every school activity, thanks to Miss Cole. Not only do we cheer at games and pep rallies, Miss Cole volunteers us to be guides on Parents' Night, to make spirit posters, and to decorate the gym for the Hops. We also bake special treats for the teams on game days.

I liked doing all of those things. But the best part was leading cheers. Getting the crowd into the game and supporting our team was a natural high.

The first night I went onto the field to cheer I was so nervous I could hardly talk. But the minute we began our yell my fear faded. The stands came alive as our team came on the field to a thunderous welcome. I felt I was a real, contributing part of Ruffner Middle School. All during the game the fans gave us what we asked for when we asked. It made all the aches, pains, long hours, and hard work worthwhile.

I sent glowing reports to Oma each week.

Even our principal was impressed. Mr. Zale turned up at one of our practice sessions. "Miss Cole, you've worked wonders," he said. "I've never seen a squad do as much so quickly and so well."

"I don't deserve the credit," Miss C. replied. "These girls are fantastic. They're very enthusiastic and dedicated."

Not everyone was always enthusiastic about every project. When Miss Cole announced the reason for our next bake-a-thon, Patsy groaned. "Why should we bake cookies for a teachers' conference?"

"Politics," Miss Cole answered. "You never know when *we* might need a favor. Trust me, girls."

We did. We baked, delivered, and served with a smile.

Mom said she might have to get a business license for the Wagner Bakery.

"You all are into everything!" Cindy said one morning. "You can't turn around without falling over a cheerleader."

"When do you find time to study?" Becca asked.

"No problems yet," I said, crossing my fingers. "I expect we'll slow down during six-weeks exams."

"You are coming with us on the hike to Laurel Point, aren't you?" Cindy asked.

"Wouldn't miss it! Am I still supposed to bring hot dogs and buns?"

Becca giggled. "Yeah. Unless you'd rather bake some cookies."

"Pul-lease!" I said, making a gagging noise. "I don't care if I never see another cookie."

"This from the girl who could down a whole batch of chocolate chips last year?"

"Funny, isn't it? Now that I don't have to count calories quite so much, I can't stand cookies. Of course, baking ninety dozen of 'em could possibly have some effect."

"I hope you don't feel that way about chocolate cake," Andrea said. "My mom's baking her Devil's Delight. It's outrageous."

"I believe you. Chocolate cake is my fave!"

Andrea's chocolate cake wasn't the only reason I was excited about the weekend. I hadn't been able to spend much time with my friends lately. My sister cheerleaders were okay, but I missed my friends. Brandy had dropped her old crowd like they were hot potatoes. I didn't want to do that. I looked forward to the long hike up to the falls, especially if Jeff was going along. I hadn't seen much of him since I'd had to change my computer class.

As I was coming out of English class, Tacy stopped me. "Can I see you for a minute, Margo?"

"Sure."

Tacy's the other captain of our squad. She's pretty but not too bright. I know because she's in the ninth grade algebra class I've been switched into.

"Could you do that horrible algebra homework?" she asked.

"Yeah. But it took forever."

"I had a splitting headache after practice. Mom made me go straight up to bed after supper. Now

61

I'm in trouble. I can't afford a zero. Can I borrow yours?"

I was so shocked I couldn't say anything. No one has ever asked to copy my whole assignment.

"Look, it's no big deal. I could have done the problems if I hadn't been sick. I didn't think you'd mind helping a sister," Tacy said.

I doubted she could have done the problems but she'd said the magic word—sister. "Okay. I guess it's all right this once."

"Thanks, Margo. All for one and one for all," she said, slipping my homework into her math book. "I'll give this back next period."

I like to help people but this just didn't feel right. It had taken me an hour and a half to do those thirty problems. Besides, why should I have to do all her work? It left a sour taste in my mouth all day.

Miss Cole finished ruining my day at our practice session. "Girls, I have some terrific news! As you know, our uniforms are somewhat worse for wear. We really need new ones and we don't have the funds to buy them. *But* . . . an anonymous donor has agreed to match any money we raise by our own efforts. Isn't that wonderful?"

"Yes!"

"And I've arranged our first money-raising venture for this Saturday."

"This Saturday?" I croaked. "Does it have to be this Saturday?"

"What's the project?" Brandy asked eagerly.

Miss Cole ignored me and answered Brandy. "First National Bank at the mall has agreed to let us use

62

their parking lot and their water for a car wash. With all of the Saturday shoppers, I'm sure we can make a bundle. How about it, squad? Are you for it?"

Everyone except me was very enthusiastic. I went along with the plans though. We do need new uniforms. Patching and cleaning my outfit keeps me and Mom busy. Sometimes I think Mom's sorry she signed those papers. She's never said a word, but I think she's more involved than she bargained for.

"Do you think some of your fathers might come to the car wash to get us started?" Miss C. asked.

"I know how to wash a car," I snapped. Playing the helpless female didn't appeal to me.

"Not all of us have your experience at those kinds of jobs," Brandy said in a sugary voice.

Tacy and Patsy volunteered to ask their fathers.

"Good! Then I'll get in touch with the local newspaper. A little publicity never hurts. Perhaps when other organizations learn of our need they'll chip in some funds."

Dad said he'd be glad to lend us some hoses, brushes, buckets, and chamois cloths.

I dreaded calling Cindy. This was the third time I'd had to back out on her.

She was disappointed but nice. "Sure, Margo. I understand. You guys do need new uniforms. You've worn the old ones so much they're getting ratty."

"Yeah. You know, I could have saved a bundle if I'd known I was going to be a cheerleader. My wardrobe could have been cut in half."

"I suppose you couldn't suggest a little conservation? Like wearing the uniforms a little less?"

"Good golly, Miss Molly! How would anyone know how active we are if we didn't dress the part? That's close to treason, Cindy."

"Oops! Sorry about that!" Cindy said, laughing. "We'll miss you, Margo. I wish you could come."

"Me, too. Think of me when you eat my slice of Devil's Delight."

"Hey! There's a bright side to everything, isn't there?" Cindy laughed.

Saturday was a beautiful day. I ached to be out in the woods, enjoying the crisp autumn smells and the company of my friends. Instead, Dad and I loaded the car and drove to Riverside Mall. From previous experience I was dressed in my grungiest outfit. So were six of the other girls. Brandy, Tacy, and Mitzi, however, had on sparkling clean uniforms.

"What's the deal?" I whispered to Patsy.

"They're going to stand out front and lure customers into our car wash."

"That figures!" God forbid, Brandy should get her hands dirty.

I'll have to admit the arrangement worked. Brandy and the others kept the cars coming. We didn't even get a break until lunch and then we had to take turns eating.

Tacy and Brandy had gone over to Wendy's and bought lunch for all of us. When my turn came Brandy handed me a tray of salad. "Miss Cole suggested this for you," she said, smiling. "Because of your weight problem, you know. I put low-cal dressing on it."

My mouth was watering for a cheeseburger. I'd

worked hard and I was starving. "Thanks." I clenched my teeth to hold back the angry words that threatened to pour out.

"I got you a diet soda, too. Eat fast. The line's backing up."

My throat was too tight to allow salad down. I forced a few bites, drank my soda, and went back to work.

I was scrubbing a tire when someone yelled, "Stand up, Margo. The newspaper photographer's here."

I stood. I forgot the hose was in my hand. The spray arched over the car and completely soaked Brandy, who was kneeling in front of the car with her Car Wash sign.

The photographer snapped the picture.

Everyone doubled over laughing—except Brandy!

Brandy dripped over to me, as mad as a wet hen. "You did that on purpose!"

"No . . . no, I didn't," I said between giggles.

"It will make a great picture," the photographer said. "Much better than a dull, posed shot."

"Of course, it will," Miss C. said soothingly. "You don't really mind, do you, Brandy?"

Brandy threw me a murderous look. But she said graciously, "Of course not! Anything for the squad."

Brandy went home to change clothes and the rest of the afternoon went peacefully. We did get one other surprise—a nice one. Some of the high school cheerleaders came by to help us. Some even brought their boyfriends, with cars to be washed.

When the day ended, we were over one hundred dollars richer. Two hundred, if you counted the matching funds.

"I'm very proud of you," Miss C. said as we dragged ourselves to our parents' waiting cars. "I have several other money-making ideas—but I promise you they won't be such hard work."

I certainly hoped not. I was pooped. I was too tired to eat my supper or call Cindy to find out about the hike. I went home, showered, and went straight to bed.

Mom shook me awake Sunday morning. "Cindy's on the phone for you."

I stumbled into the hall. "Hello, Cindy. What's up?"

"Wow! You're something else, Margo! I can't believe you did it!"

"Did what?" I asked grumpily over my growling stomach.

"Haven't you seen the paper?"

"I hardly ever read the paper in my sleep, Cindy."

"Well, go get it! Look at the front page of the local news."

Joel was coming upstairs with a grin on his face. He handed me the paper. "Way to go, Sis!"

Splashed across the paper was our picture. The caption read: "Cheerleaders Wash More Than Cars For New Uniforms." Brandy looked like a drowned rat.

I laughed so hard I nearly wet my pjs.

"Isn't that worth being dragged out of bed?" Cindy asked.

"It was an accident." I tried to explain how it happened.

"Whatever!" Cindy said. "It's the best picture of

Brandy I've ever seen. I'm going to cut it out and put it up on my locker."

"Don't you dare!"

"Okay. In my room then," Cindy conceded. "You're forgiven for deserting us when you can pull off a stunt like this."

"I tell you, it was an accident."

"No way. It was justice."

I protested some more but it was useless. I wondered how Brandy felt when she saw the picture.

Chapter 8

Sisters

I walked to school Monday morning. I wanted to see Brandy without a crowd around so I waited for her outside the school entrance.

Brandy got out of her dad's car with a cheerleader smile on her face.

I went down the walk to meet her. "I'm sorry, Brandy. It really was an accident," I said humbly.

"Forget it. I suppose pictures like that sell newspapers," Brandy replied. The smile never left her face but it didn't quite reach her eyes.

"I wouldn't do a thing like that on purpose. I know how it feels to have people laughing at you."

"I suppose *you* do," Brandy snapped. She hurried past me into the building.

What else could I say after I said I was sorry? It had been an accident whether anyone believed me or not. So why was I on a guilt trip? As I walked to my locker my cheerleader smile was definitely absent. And I didn't care.

"Well, well! If it isn't the miracle worker!" Andrea said, thumping me on the back.

I was fighting my usual morning battle with my locker. It never sticks any other time. I think it likes to sleep late. "What's that supposed to mean—what has Margo done now?" Cindy asked.

"She's a miracle worker. She turned water into Wine, didn't she?" Andrea said, grinning from ear to ear.

Cindy and I looked at her blankly.

Andrea shook her head. "You girls haven't been going to Sunday school, have you? Don't you remember the miracle of turning water into wine at the wedding feast—in the Bible?"

Cindy burst out laughing. "I love it! Andrea, you're too much!"

I turned bright red. "Cut it out, Andrea. That's, uh, sacrilegious. Besides, I didn't do it on purpose."

"Still turned water into Wine," Andrea mumbled, trying to keep a straight face.

I grinned in spite of myself. It's hard to stay hacked with Andrea.

"You better watch your back, Margo," Andrea warned, soberly. "You keep in mind what Brandy did to Cindy last year."

"Don't be silly. Brandy and I are sister cheerleaders. She just had her pride wounded a little."

"Yeah. But that's the biggest part of her."

Andrea's warning stayed with me. It made me a little nervous about going to practice. What if the rest of the girls—and Miss Cole—felt the way Brandy did?

Miss Cole's announcement put me at ease. "Squad,

69

it seems people do read captions under funny pictures. We have received two hundred dollars in donations toward our new uniforms after our picture ran in Sunday's paper."

A cheer, followed by a collective sigh of relief, rose from the group. We thought that was the end of our money-making projects.

Miss C. was quick to set us straight. "Now, girls, that doesn't mean we're out of the woods yet. We still need about two hundred dollars more if we want to purchase first class uniforms."

"We do!" Brandy and Mitzi said in unison.

Miss C. waited until we all nodded our agreement. "Good. I do have some news I'm sure you'll welcome. There will be no practice sessions during six-weeks exams. You may use this PE period to study."

"Thank goodness," Lori muttered. "I'm really behind in history and English."

"One more item," Miss C. said, raising her voice over the excited buzz. "It has come to my attention that some of you are not behaving very charitably toward your sisters."

The room grew very quiet.

"I find this very difficult to believe. I've told you that nothing meant more to me in college than winning the championship trophy. Well, that isn't the exact truth. What meant more was knowing I had friends I could count on. Our squad was closer than sisters. There wasn't anything we wouldn't do for one another. That's what it takes to win championships. Dedication to each other. And to cheerleading. I thought you had that. Now I'm not

70

certain." Her bachelor button blue eyes were misting over. She looked so disappointed and miserable.

It was awful! We all admired Miss Cole. We wanted to please her. Secretly, I think most of us wanted to be just like her. She's so pretty, so together, so with it. All the guys in school, including the male teachers, fall all over themselves trying to be cool when she's around. And here we were making her cry.

Mitzi broke the guilty silence. "We are dedicated, Miss Cole! We'll help each other, won't we girls?"

My "Yes!" was louder than all the rest. I felt more guilt. I'd refused to let Tacy copy my math homework again. And, after Barby had "borrowed" my book report and my science outline, I'd said no to her third request. Maybe I had been selfish.

"That's the spirit! Remember, if you fail even one subject, you're suspended from the team. We've worked too hard on our routines to mess up our squad now. So hit those books, gang! Each one help one," Miss Cole said with her beautiful smile back in place.

We practiced very hard for the rest of the period. I felt good about helping Lori, Patsy, and Tacy with their math. I think I got through to Patsy and Lori. I had doubts about Tacy. Borrowing other people's homework instead of doing it herself hadn't helped her—except to get a good daily grade.

"If you want to come over to my house tonight, I'll help you review," I said to Tacy when the last bell rang.

"No thanks. I'm going to a movie. I have a date," Tacy replied.

71

"On a school night?"

"Sure. Why not?"

I blushed. "My folks won't let me go out unless it's a school function."

"Get real! That's Dark Ages stuff. I'll bet your brothers get to do as they please."

"No, they don't."

Tacy smirked at me. "You may be good in math but you don't know the score in your own house, Margo. I saw Joel at the movies last Wednesday with Brenda Phillips. Looks like what you have is a double standard at your place. Ask Joel if you don't believe me."

I knew Joel was dating Brenda but I couldn't believe he'd break our family rules. "I will ask him!"

"I have a better idea," Tacy said. "Save this little tidbit until you need it. Sometimes a little black-mail comes in handy. Believe me, I know. I have two older sisters and a brother."

I watched, with my mouth hanging open, as Tacy swished down the hall. I couldn't imagine black-mailing anyone, much less one of my brothers.

"Hey, Margo. You okay?"

I looked up. Jeff was staring down at me with a look of concern on his face. "Just daydreaming," I said, starting toward my locker.

Jeff loped along with me. "You missed a good hike Saturday."

"So I heard. I guess you saw in the papers where I was."

"Your picture didn't do you justice," he said, smiling.

"Didn't do anyone justice!" I replied. "But it did get us some donations for our new uniforms." I love Jeff's smile! Most of the time he has a dreamy, serious look, but when he smiles he's awesome. "How's it going? I haven't seen much of you since I changed computer classes."

"I'm out of there, too," he said, blushing to the roots of his blond curls. "I go over to the high school for class now."

"I kinda thought the class might be too easy for you. How's the high school class?"

"All right, I guess. They have more equipment but they're cramped for space. It'll be better when they move to the new building."

Instead of going on toward the buses, Jeff waited while I collected my books. When I started for my bus instead of the gym, Jeff said, "Hey, don't you have practice?"

"Nope. Miss C. Let us off during exams."

"Time off for good behavior, huh?"

"Not exactly," I replied, feeling a twinge of guilt. "Some people need time to study. We have to pass every subject to stay on the squad."

Jeff flashed me another awesome smile. "*You* don't need to worry. Wanna go down to High's for a sundae? I got my first paycheck yesterday."

Jeff's invitation erased all thoughts of guilt, double standards, blackmail, and exams from my head. "Sure. That sounds super. Did you get a paper route?"

Jeff blushed again. "No, I work for my dad in our Sport Store. I'm a stock boy. And in my spare time I'm putting our whole inventory into our computer."

"Wow! Neat!"

73

"Yeah. I like the job and the money. But it only gives me one Saturday off a month. Here, let me carry those books. You've cleaned out your locker."

"Miss Cole has kept us pretty busy these six weeks. I need to review in every subject."

"Cindy said you'd been awfully busy. How do you like cheerleading?"

It was strange but no one had ever asked me that question. I guess everyone assumed if you made cheerleader you had it made. Jeff asked as if he really cared how I felt. It made me collect my thoughts before I answered him.

Talking with Jeff was so easy. We talked our way through a Triple Delight and were still going strong when I noticed the time. "Gosh! I've got to go. It's almost dinner time."

"If we hurry you can catch the five o'clock bus," Jeff said, grabbing some of my stuff.

We made it to the city bus stop as the bus came around the corner. "Thanks for the sundae."

Jeff handed me my books. "Thank Cindy. She said if I wanted to see you I'd have to make an effort."

"I'm glad you did," I said, feeling my face go red and my heart race madly.

"See you tomorrow."

The smile on my face was a genuine, happy smile. People on the bus smiled back at me. For the moment everything and everybody seemed wonderful and happy.

My mother was not happy. She was getting out of the car as I ambled up the walk. "Where have you been, Margo? I've been worried sick."

"I went to High's for a sundae—with Jeff Johnson," I answered dreamily.

"Well, don't you ever do this to me again!" Mom stormed. "You are supposed to call me if you don't have practice and are going anywhere. Otherwise, you are to come straight home after school."

"I'm sorry. I forgot."

"Well, don't you forget again! I've been calling all over trying to find you."

Mom marched into the house, throwing her car keys on the counter.

"What's the big deal? It's the middle of the afternoon, Mom. Did you think I'd been kidnapped or something?" I asked, trying to keep the irritation out of my voice.

Mom turned on me angrily. "Young lady, we have a rule in this house. We let one another know where we're going. I want to know where my children are—all of the time."

"I don't remember Joel and Frank checking in every five minutes."

"Joel and Frank are older. Besides, they're boys. We are discussing your lack of consideration," Mom snapped.

"I don't call this discussing. I call it getting reamed out . . . and a double standard!"

I pushed past her and marched up to my room. Mom and I had never had a real fight before. Sure, I was wrong not to call her but she was treating me like a baby. A thirteen-year-old deserves some freedom. Tacy was right. There is a double standard at my house. And it isn't fair!

Chapter 9

All for One and One for All

Mom and I made up but it was an uneasy truce.

I apologized for snapping at her and for forgetting to call her about the cancelled practice.

Mom explained that she was upset about a report of a girl being raped in Maymount Park the night before.

Personally, I thought that was a pretty lame excuse for her behavior. I had been nowhere near Maymount Park. And it was broad daylight, for heaven's sake! Joel and Frank come and go as they please just because they're boys!

It didn't even help when I found out Cindy's and Becca's moms were just as uptight. I still felt resentful. I didn't talk to Mom very much anymore.

All ten cheerleaders made it through the six-weeks exams. Tacy got a *C*- in algebra and was as proud of it as if it had been an *A*.

Miss Cole was in a proper tizzy after our enforced

vacation. "Girls, football and soccer seasons are almost over and basketball season is upon us. We got away with many mistakes because we were so far from the crowd. Basketball changes that. Every error will be in full view—of the audience *and* our competition. Ruffner has the opportunity to shine or be disgraced.

"During our break I was able to observe the Leland Middle School cheerleaders. *They* didn't take time off. I feel they will be our stiffest competition. In fact, if the competition were held now they'd beat us hands down. Fortunately, we have until March to get our act together. That may sound a long time away but remember we have Thanksgiving and Christmas breaks."

"Leland's our biggest rival in everything," Mitzi complained.

"They usually beat us, too," Tacy added. "I'd love to cream 'em!"

There were murmurs of agreement from all of us.

"Would you be willing to have a few extra Saturday and Sunday practices then? I think we can rub their noses in the dirt—if we put out a little extra effort," Miss Cole said.

The prospect of beating Leland put enthusiasm into our, "Yes!"

Miss C.'s eyes glittered happily. "Good! I know some neat new formations that my squad used in college last year. If we can master these we'll really knock their socks off! Are you willing to try?"

Our response was deafening in the small practice room.

"This will mean a lot of intense work."

77

"We don't care!" yelled Brandy. "We want to win that championship!"

Miss Cole looked at us with fierce pride. "Huddle!"

We formed a circle with our arms around each other and on the count of three yelled, "All for one and one for all!"

From then on we had practice every day in school, three times a week after school, and on Saturday and Sunday. These were in addition to our regular appearances at school functions and our fund-raising activities.

"Don't you ever do anything else?" Cindy complained. She had invited me to go to the Saturday matinee with the gang and I'd had to say no.

"We're going to beat Leland! Just you wait and see."

"Well, I'd like that. But I'd also like to see a little more of you. I'm not the only one who feels that way either," Cindy said pointedly.

"I know. I'd like to spend more time with you guys, too. But, like Miss C. says, if you want to be champions you have to make some sacrifices."

"Yeah. I guess."

"After the movie why don't you come down to the mall? We're having a bake sale. I've made my chocolate chip brownies."

"Maybe we will. If we're not too full of popcorn and junk."

"Save a space. Support your local cheerleaders. We need those new uniforms."

"What are they going to be made of—solid gold? You've had more fund-raisers than a dog has fleas," Cindy said grumpily.

"Now you sound like my mom. She said yesterday that she'd rather *buy* the new uniforms. But not everyone can afford to do that. So we rake, bake, wash, and sell."

"Have fun," Cindy said and hung up.

Our hard work was paying off. Each week we learned new routines. The spectators began to expect something different at every game. Their applause was wonderful. I loved it!

The dangerous and difficult pyramid with Patsy doing a back flip from the top brought everyone to their feet. We did that one for half-time at the Leland game. The Leland cheerleaders practically turned green. No junior high cheerleaders had ever attempted that formation. We felt great!

Just before our Thanksgiving break Miss C. announced, "Good news, squad! We've gone over the top. We have enough money for our new uniforms. I'm ordering them today."

When the cheering died down Brandy stood up. "And to celebrate I'm throwing a party Saturday night. Don't worry. You won't have to bake anything. This will be catered!"

We laughed and cheered.

"And since the high school cheerleaders have been so supportive of our efforts we've decided to invite them," Miss C. added.

"How about some guys?" asked Tacy.

"Of course!" Miss C. said, laughing. "A hen party wouldn't be much fun. Each girl ask a guy."

Lori was sitting beside me. She didn't look very

happy. "I don't know any boys who'd fit in," she whispered. "Who are you going to ask?"

"Jeff Johnson," I answered promptly. "But I'm sure you don't have to ask anyone. It will be just one big gang of kids."

Patsy came hurrying over to confer with Lori about the same problem. Most seventh graders don't do a lot of dating. The girls may be ready but the boys sure aren't.

"Why don't the two of you come together?" I suggested. "Ask Miss Cole. I'm sure it will be okay."

Looking relieved, Patsy and Lori went to talk with Miss C.

After practice Tacy came over to my locker. She's been pretty cool toward me all these six weeks. She and Brandy have become big buddies. "Are you asking anyone to Brandy's party, Margo?"

"Yes, Jeff Johnson."

Tacy's face fell about a mile. "Oh, no!"

"What's wrong with Jeff?"

"Nothing. It's just that I had a favor to ask."

"What's the favor?"

"It doesn't matter. Not if you're going to ask Jeff."

"I haven't asked him yet, for heaven's sake. What's the favor?"

Tacy's face brightened a little. "We were trying to do something nice for someone. You know Brandy and I have been dating these high school guys—Logan Rogers and Bill Tranter?"

I nodded. That little item was not secret. Tacy and Brandy had made certain of that.

"Well," Tacy continued, "Bill and Logan have a

best friend, Kenny Price. You probably remember him from our last bake sale. He bought almost all of your brownies. And not because he likes brownies. You get my drift?"

I blushed and nodded. I remembered the guy. He'd been my best customer. In fact I hadn't had any brownies left when Cindy and Becca came by. I'd thought he just liked brownies.

"Kenny's real shy around girls. Bill and Logan were trying to help him out. They asked if you'd invite Kenny to the party. We said we thought you would because you liked to help people. It wouldn't be a real date, just the six of us hanging around together. You could see that Kenny doesn't go off in a corner by himself."

"He's really shy, huh?"

"You're the first girl he's shown any interest in, Bill says. Kenny thinks girls won't like him because he's so big and awkward."

"He didn't seem awkward to me. And he isn't any bigger than my brothers."

"I know," Tacy said, sighing. "Kenny just thinks he's big and awkward. Know what I mean?"

Sure, I knew. I was a trim size eight now but sometimes I still felt fat. Sometimes your brain doesn't believe what it sees in the mirror. I knew exactly where Kenny was coming from. "Okay. I'll do it."

"You will? Oh, geez! That's terrific," Tacy said, hugging me. "You're a real sport, Margo."

Sport or not, there was one thing I knew I'd better find out before I went home with the party news. I practically threw on the rest of my clothes.

81

Brandy has a reputation in the party department; last year her bashes were the talk of the school. Not only because they were so lavish but because her parents were usually absent and something wild always happened. My parents knew about Brandy's parties. I was certain-sure they wouldn't let me go if no adults were going to be there.

I caught up with Brandy and Tacy was they were leaving the gym. "This party sounds neat, Brandy. I'm dying to see your house and meet your parents."

"My parents are anxious to meet all of my nine sisters, too," Brandy said, laughing. "Daddy even cancelled a trip to Chicago so he can be there. I sure hope everybody comes."

"Miss Cole is going to invite her boyfriend," Tacy added. "This is going to be some party!"

They had answered my concerns. We were certainly going to be well chaperoned.

"Thanks for helping out with Kenny, Margo," Brandy said. "Could I ask one more favor? Would you help me plan this party? My mom tends to go overboard."

"Sure." I was flattered. Brandy rarely asked my opinion on anything.

Mom was waiting for me in the car with a big smile on her face. "What's up?" I asked.

"I have good news. Oma and Opa are coming for Thanksgiving."

"Super! When are they coming?"

"Next Wednesday. And they're staying until Saturday."

"Wow! That's a first. How'd you get Opa away from the farm for that long?"

"Your father did some tall talking. Mr. Beecher's going to look after things. It's the longest they've been away from the place in years."

"I have some good news, too. We finally have enough money for our uniforms. Miss Cole ordered them today."

"Hallelujah! No more bake sales!"

"No more tatty uniforms to get cleaned every other day."

"My oven and my washing machine thank you," Mom said, laughing.

"Brandy's giving a party for the cheerleaders Saturday night." I slipped it in while she was in a good mood.

Mom turned to look at me, taking her eyes off the road. "Brandy's giving a party?"

"Look where you're going!" I shouted.

Mom jerked the car back into the proper lane. A car behind us honked rudely.

"Don't shout at me, Margo," Mom said testily. "You'll have to decline the invitation."

"Why? We'll be well chaperoned. Mr. and Mrs. Wine will be there. So will Miss Cole and her boyfriend."

"And how do you know this?"

"I asked. I knew you'd object. I knew you'd remember last year. I just knew you'd treat me like a baby!"

"Margo Wagner! What a thing to say!" Mom exclaimed, pulling crookedly into our driveway.

I don't know why I was being so mean. But I couldn't stop. "You don't want me to have any fun.

You just want me to be 'fat little Margo,' your baby girl."

Mom looked as if I'd slapped her face. "That isn't true, Margo. What on earth has gotten into you?"

"All I know is you don't forbid Joel and Frank going to parties! They *never* had to have chaperones. They get to have fun. All I ever get is grief. You don't trust me!"

I jumped out of the car, slammed the door, and marched into the house. Even when I said those awful things I knew I wasn't being fair. But I couldn't help myself.

I went straight up to my room. I wished I had someone to talk to about how I felt. I wanted to call Cindy but I knew *positively* that she wouldn't understand. We'd had too many discussions about Brandy's parties. The first thing Cindy would want to know was why I even wanted to go. The second thing she'd ask was why I hadn't invited Jeff. Both questions were hard to answer. The best I could come up with was that I wanted to be one of the gang. I've always felt just a little out of step with the rest of the squad—somehow a member of the team but not a part of it. I guess I hoped if I did this favor and helped with the party I'd really be accepted. Try explaining that to anyone. It's too corny.

Dinner that night was very tense. Mom looked as if she'd been crying. Dad looked angry. I was pouting. Frank and Joel read the signs and were quiet.

I felt rotten. After dinner, when Mom and I were silently cleaning up, I got up enough nerve to say, "I'm sorry, Mom. I didn't mean all the things I said. I'm just cranky lately."

Mom stopped loading the dishwasher and looked me straight in the eye. "I've never known you to be so hateful or unfair, Margo. You hurt my feelings."

"I'm really sorry, Mom, but you hurt my feelings, too."

"I'm sorry, too. I'm sorry you feel the way you do. And I'm sorry I refused to let you go to the party without listening to what you had to say. Part of your complaints are justified. We do have different rules for the boys. We try to be fair, but sometimes we can't seem to forget you're our baby girl. We don't, however, wish to keep you a baby or keep you from having fun. We want you to grow up safe, healthy, and happy. That's our responsibility as parents."

I hung my head. "I know that," I said to my toes.

Mom came over, tilted my chin up and kissed me on the forehead. "Just so you understand, Margo. In spite of my behavior today, you can always talk to us. Let's go tell your father about your new uniforms. And your party."

Arm in arm we went into the den. I was cautious though. I didn't mention about any boys coming to the party. Or my "date" with Kenny Price. I already knew how they felt about girls dating so early.

Dad agreed to let me go to the party if I promised to be in by eleven o'clock and if I would be certain to behave responsibly.

"Eleven's fine. And you know you can count on me. I always keep a cool head."

Chapter 10

The Party

"How come you didn't ask Jeff?"

News of Brandy's party had spread through Ruffner like wildfire. Cindy was reacting as I had predicted.

"I haven't personally asked anyone. I'm sorta helping plan this celebration," I replied. That was the truth, if not the whole truth. "Besides, I didn't think Jeff would like it."

"Why not?"

"Well, most of the girls are inviting jocks, you know. Jeff isn't into the athletic scene."

Cindy gave me a funny look. "Oh, I see."

"No, you don't! I want to ask Jeff but I don't want him to feel out of place. Can't you think of some nice way to tell him that for me?"

A mulish look slid over Cindy's face. "I don't see how I can. It doesn't sound very nice to me. Either you like Jeff or you don't."

"I do like Jeff! I just don't want to ask him to this one party. I can't."

"You *can't?* Are your cheerleader sisters picking out your friends now?"

I blushed. "Not really. I'm doing a favor for someone, that's all."

"Oh, well, that's different. Anything goes for a sister, I guess."

"Cindy, please . . ."

Cindy sighed. "Okay. I'll try to explain it to Jeff—even if *I* don't understand."

"Thanks." That really took a load off my mind—my conscience, too.

Brandy, Tacy, and I spent every spare minute together during the week, planning the party. Brandy wanted my ideas on everything from the decorations to the food.

"I want this party to be exactly right," she confided. "After all, we're having a lot of high school kids . . . people who'll be our classmates next year. We don't want to get off on the wrong foot . . . like I did last year."

"It's going to be a smash," I assured her. "We have plenty of food, good music, and a bunch of kids who have a lot in common. What more do we need?"

"I just want everything to be perfect. I want everyone to have a good time. You will take care of Kenny, won't you? Bill and Logan won't have any fun if Kenny's miserable."

"Sure. I won't let him go off in a corner by himself. I'll go with him," I said with more confidence than I felt. Heck, I'd probably be more nervous than Kenny. But I did feel better about being with Kenny after Cindy talked with Jeff. Jeff had said he wouldn't have gone to Brandy's party anyway.

87

I was a basket case by the time Dad dropped me off at Brandy's house Saturday night. I'd changed clothes six times. I was a little late.

"This is quite an estate," Dad observed as he drove around the curved driveway.

It was impressive. The house was set back from the road, surrounded by trees and lit up like the State Capitol or something.

My mouth was dry. "Thanks for the ride, Dad. I'll call if I need a way home."

"Eleven o'clock is curfew," he reminded me. "Have a good time, Margo."

I got out of the car and watched as he drove off. I didn't know whether to go up to the front door or down the lighted brick path at the side of the house. I decided on the front door.

A maid in a black uniform and a frilly white apron answered the chimes. I only got glimpses of the house as I followed her down the hall. It was awesome! The hall floors were black marble. The sunken living room had a huge stone fireplace and a carpet that looked six inches deep. Everything looked brand new ... like no one lived here. It looked more like a museum than a home.

"Down the stairs, through the door, Miss," the maid said as the chimes sounded again.

I couldn't hear a sound as I approached the door. I thought maybe I'd come too early. But when I opened the heavy door, stereo music nearly knocked me off my feet.

"There you are!" Brandy cried over the loud din. "Let me take your jacket. Come meet my parents." She grabbed my arm and led me toward a distinguished-looking man in a three piece suit and a woman in a slinky black dress.

"This is Margo Wagner, the tenth member of our squad," Brandy said.

"Delighted to meet you," Mr. Wine said formally. "Congratulations on meeting your goal."

"We're always happy to meet Brandy's friends," a perfectly made-up Mrs. Wine gushed, smiling. "Miss Cole tells us you are going to win the State Championship."

"We're sure going to try."

"Come on," Brandy urged. "Kenny's already here. I want you to get acquainted before we eat."

We wove our way through some dancing couples into another room.

"This is the game room," Brandy explained unnecessarily.

I was surrounded by a ping-pong table, a pool table, and two video games. All were occupied.

"That's Kenny over there playing Space Invaders. I'll introduce you," Brandy said, dragging me along.

Even from across the room Kenny looked huge. He must be over six feet tall and all muscle, I thought. I felt dainty and petite when I stood beside him and Brandy introduced us.

"Hey, Margo. I've heard a lot about you," he said. "Want to challenge me to a game?"

"Sure. I'm not very good at video games though. I probably won't be much competition."

"I'll teach you. I'm good at playing games." He winked at Brandy and me.

"Well, I'm willing to try anything once."

Kenny laughed. "Hey, now! You're my kind of girl!"

I smiled back. So far, so good, I thought.

"I'll see you all later," Brandy said. "I have to go play hostess."

"How long before we eat?" asked Kenny.

"As soon as everyone arrives. You'll have time to work up an appetite," Brandy said.

"We don't need to work up one, do we, Margo?" Kenny said, dropping a massive arm over my shoulder.

"I can always eat. Show me how to play this game," I said, almost collapsing under the weight of his arm.

We played two games, which Kenny won, before Brandy came through announcing dinner.

We went into yet another room which had a long buffet table simply groaning with food. Ten small tables, each set for four people, were scattered around. A blue banner was strung across the back of the room. Big white letters proclaimed WE'RE ON OUR WAY.

"How do you like the banner?" Brandy asked. "Miss Cole made it for us."

"Super!" I wondered what had happened to the crepe paper streamers I'd suggested.

Kenny and I made our way down the buffet line. His plate was piled high and he kept urging things on me. "Have to keep up your strength," he said. "I don't date girls who're always on a diet."

I didn't think he dated girls at all. Maybe he was just being macho. Besides it was hard to pass up

anything on that table, especially the spiced shrimp.
I go ape over shrimp. I took a double helping.

With our plates loaded, we made our way to a
vacant table. That's when I noticed that everyone
was in pairs. Everyone, that is, except Lori and
Patsy who were coming through the line looking
fearfully out of place. I waved and motioned for
them to join us.

"Why'd you do that?" Kenny growled.

"Because they're seventh graders and they didn't
ask any guys." Surely, I thought, being a shy person he can understand that.

"The blond's kinda cute," Kenny allowed.

"That's Patsy. She's one of our best cheerleaders."

"Yeah?" Kenny said and dived into his food.

"Can you believe this place?" Lori asked after I
made the introductions.

"I can't believe this food!" Patsy said. "You girls
did a super job on the buffet." Her plate was as full
as Kenny's.

"I can't take any credit for this," I said. "This
spread isn't anything like what Tacy, Brandy, and I
planned. Mrs. Wine must have done this."

"Whoever!" Patsy said. She and Kenny cleaned
their plates and went back for seconds.

While we were waiting for the desserts to be
brought out Miss Cole stood up and made a little
speech. "Mr. and Mrs. Wine, we want to thank you
for such a lovely party. We certainly didn't expect
anything so magnificent. We also want to thank
the high school cheerleaders for coming tonight. We
feel you are our big sisters and we thank you for

91

your generous support. We hope to make you proud of us by winning the State Junior Championship!"

She sat down to loud cheers.

Mr. Wine rose and bowed slightly to Miss Cole. "We are delighted to entertain champions. I love winners. I agree with the coach who said 'winning isn't everything—it's the *only* thing.' That is my philosophy. So go for the gold! The silver and bronze aren't worth your effort."

After that speech I could sure see where Brandy got her desire to win.

A few people ate desserts and then we drifted back toward the other rooms. Kenny and I talked with a few kids while we waited for our turn at Donkey Kong.

"Let's go dance," Kenny suggested, since the line for the game didn't seem to be moving.

Patsy and Lori were just leaving when we walked into the room full of dancing couples. I couldn't blame them. I knew they felt out of place. Evidently our chaperones felt out of place, too. Mr. and Mrs. Wine, Miss Cole, and her date had vanished.

"I wonder where the Wines are?" I said.

"Upstairs where they belong," Kenny said, grabbing me in a bear hug. "Now we can get down and party."

I started to say I wasn't a very good dancer but I couldn't say anything. My face was mashed against Kenny's shirt.

Three or four dances later I was as limp as a dishrag and as dry as a desert. "Let's sit this one out," I croaked.

"I'll get you some punch. That'll pick you up."

I hardly had time to catch my breath before he was back with the punch. I gulped down a huge glass of the raunchy-tasting mixture and we were off again. One thing for sure, Kenny wasn't shy about dancing.

Kenny and I were still dancing when I was rescued by Logan. He came up and whispered something in Kenny's ear and Kenny let go of me. I was delighted because I was getting dizzy from lack of air. Kenny's idea of slow dancing was to hold me in a vise-grip and sway to the music.

"The movie's about to start. Let's go," Kenny said.

"What movie?"

"They're showing a special video in the entertainment room. Come on," Kenny said, grinning.

"I hope it's cooler in there. This room's awfully warm."

Kenny thought my remark was very funny for some reason.

"I want to sit down. I don't feel very well," I said when we reached the darkened room.

"Sit right here with me, babe," Kenny said, pulling me down on the couch beside him.

I sank down and closed my eyes. My stomach was doing funny little flip-flops. "It's the shrimp swimming around," I said, giggling.

I tried to watch the movie but I was having trouble with my eyes. Kenny was having trouble with his hands. They kept landing in the strangest places. I kept moving them.

I must have dozed off for a minute because when I looked at the TV screen again I thought I saw a bunch of naked people all tangled up. I'm not really certain what I saw because my stomach gave a lurch and I jumped up, pulling Kenny with me. "Outside," I managed to gasp.

"Right," Kenny said. "I like privacy, too."

We went through the sliding doors into the pool area. The cold air felt wonderful. I took a deep breath, trying to calm my stomach.

Kenny grabbed me in another vise-grip and tried to kiss me!

I pushed him away . . . but not in time. My dinner came up like something shot from a slingshot.

Kenny dodged but he lost his balance and fell into the pool.

I screamed.

Thank goodness, Brandy and Logan were nearby. Kenny was floundering around like a walrus. There was no way I could pull him out by myself. I tried but he kept flopping back in.

Brandy and Logan fished him out.

Kenny was furious. "I thought you said this chick was hot-to-trot, Brandy! She's colder than an iceberg," he bellowed.

"Shut up, Kenny!" Brandy ordered.

It was as if someone had thrown cold water in my face. Suddenly all the odd events of the evening— the sly winks, the funny tasting punch, the roving hands—all made sense. I didn't wait to hear any more. I slipped out of the gathering crowd and started home. What I really wanted to do was crawl in a hole and die.

No such luck for stupid Margo. I was alive, sick,

94

cold, and at least two miles from home. Never in all my life had I felt like such a jerk.

I jogged along as fast as I could, jumping into the shadows whenever I heard a car approaching. Brandy was sure to send someone out looking for me. The last thing I wanted was to see anyone from that crowd.

At the corner of Broad and Regent I looked at my watch. It was ten-thirty! I only had a half hour until curfew. I'd never make it, not stopping and hiding every time a car came by.

Maymount Park loomed ahead of me. The November-naked trees looked like skeleton arms waiting to grab anyone who dared enter. The thought of the girl who'd been raped also crossed my mind. But at this point I didn't care who or what grabbed me as long as it wasn't anyone from the party. I entered the park at a full gallop. It would shave fifteen minutes off my journey.

I made it to my front steps with five minutes to spare just as a car pulled to the curb.

"Margo! Wait!" Tacy shouted.

"Goodnight!" I called and dashed inside.

"Have to go to the bathroom," I said to Mom and Dad as I ran down the hall. "Back in a minute to tell you about the party."

I did have to go. But mostly I wanted to clean up and pull myself together before I faced them. I ached to go in and pour out my hurt like I did when I was a little girl. There was no way I could do that now. I'd promised to behave responsibly and I'd been a *dummkopf.* They would probably be more ashamed of me than I was of myself. If they ever found out about tonight they wouldn't let me out of the house until I was an old lady of twenty-five.

I straightened my clothes, washed my face, and went out and told the biggest lie of my life.

"It was a wonderful party!"

Chapter 11

Cover-Up

"Brandy and Tacy are here to see you. They're returning your jacket," Mom announced, sticking her head into my room Sunday afternoon.

Saying Russia had dropped the bomb couldn't have made me feel much worse. I thought I'd have at least one day before I had to face those rats. I closed the book I'd been pretending to read. "Send them up."

"You forgot your jacket," Brandy said, bouncing into my room with a bright smile pasted on her face.

Tacy wasn't quite so good an actress. Worry showed through her fake smile as she closed my door.

Brandy held out my jacket. When I didn't take it, she tossed it on the bed. "I'm sorry, Margo. It was just a harmless joke. It was supposed to be funny . . . pairing you with the high school's number one lover-boy, I mean."

"I'm not laughing."

Brandy hung her head. "I know. The joke back-fired. Logan didn't tell me the truth about Kenny. I never would have set you up with him if I'd known he was such an animal."

"I'm not buying that, Brandy. It was a lousy trick. You led me on, asking me to help plan the party, wanting my opinion on everything. Why'd you do it? I thought we were supposed to be sisters."

"You made me look foolish at the car wash. I was just getting even."

"Are you going to fink on us?" Tacy demanded.

"We've covered everything up," Brandy put in hastily. "Everyone thinks you just got sick and that Kenny slipped. You ran away because you were embarrassed about the fuss."

"So? What's to fink about? You're in the clear."

"Don't be dense!" Tacy said. "You know we're talking about the booze and the porno flick."

"If that ever comes out both cheerleading squads are in big trouble. Mr. Zale would probably disband us! You don't want that, do you?" Brandy asked, pleading with her big brown eyes. "Adults are so uptight when kids do the same things they do all the time. It's so hypocritical! It's like saying you have to be a certain age to have fun. Besides, Margo, not everyone was drinking and not everyone saw the movie. But if this comes out everyone will be hurt."

Brandy had me cornered. She knew I wouldn't want to be branded a baby and a fink. It was better to swallow my hurt feelings than to have everyone punished. "Okay. I'm not going to blow the whistle on your fun and games. But you'd better not pull another stunt like this again—*ever*."

"We won't," Tacy and Brandy said solemnly.

They had gotten what they had come for.

I heaved a sigh of relief when they left. I thought the worst was over for today. I was wrong.

A few minutes later, without even knocking, Joel burst into my room and slammed the door. He glared at me. "I heard about that party last night," he hissed. "Have you told Mom and Dad?"

"About what?" I asked, putting on my best innocent expression.

"Cut it out, Margo! It won't wash. You know I'm talking about booze and dirty movies at a middle school party."

"And you've never heard of booze at a party?"

Joel flushed. "That's beside the point. Some high school kids are jerks and the operative word here is *high school*."

"That's two words."

"Whatever! Margo, all the guys at the Rec Center were talking about your wild party. Word is out that we've got a hot group coming up next year. And this hot group includes my little sister! I think Mom and Dad ought to know what's going down at these parties you're going to."

"You weren't there. How do you know what went on? You're just trying to make trouble, Joel."

"*I'm* not the one making trouble."

"Yes, you are. You're spreading a rumor. I could spread some rumors myself—if *I* want to make trouble."

"Like what?"

"Like who says he's going to work on a school project on a Wednesday night and instead takes his girl to the movies? I heard that happened. But I don't *know* that it did."

A guilty flash rose on Joel's cheeks. "That's blackmail. What's gotten into you, Margo? I didn't think you were that kind of person. You keep on like this and you're headed for big trouble."

Joel was looking at me like I was some sort of disgusting bug. "Butt out, Joel," I said wearily. "I can take care of myself."

Joel turned on his heels and stormed out. He slammed the door so hard my calendar fell off the wall.

I felt lower than a blacksnake's belly. So far this week I'd been suckered by people I thought were my friends, had a fight with my mother, guzzled spiked punch, barfed on my date, lied to my parents, agreed to a cover-up, and blackmailed my favorite brother. I didn't like me very much.

Monday was even worse than I expected. Everyone wanted to know about the party I wanted to forget. I got by with describing Brandy's house, the decorations, and the food. What I couldn't handle was the teasing from my sister cheerleaders. It was clear Brandy and Tacy had not kept silent.

"Went off your bland diet, huh, Margo?"

"Are you and Kenny trying out for the swim team next year?"

"Nah-h. I heard they were going out for parts in the play *Close Encounters.*"

"Really? I heard it was the *Barfsville Horror.*"

"Yuck! You gross me out."

Patsy and Lori were the only ones who didn't take part in the locker room ribbing. They'd left the party before the action began.

I tried to be a good sport and laugh at their jokes but I felt rotten inside.

Only Cindy noticed any difference in me. "You're beginning to look like the others. What's the matter, Margo?"

"What do you mean?"

Cindy shrugged into her coat and kicked her locker shut. "You're wearing a fake smile. Have been all week. What's eating you?"

Oh, how I wanted to tell her! That was one of the worst things about this whole business. I didn't have anyone to talk with. I smiled—convincingly, I hope. "Nothing's wrong. I'm just tired. We're putting in double practices again because of the holidays and second six-weeks exams."

"Yeah. Well, if you ever want to talk, you know my number. Have a happy Thanksgiving. Say 'hi' to Oma for me," Cindy said and ran to catch her bus.

I've never felt so alone as I felt right at that moment, standing in the middle of a hall full of people. The dam of the Wagner Waterworks threatened to burst. I swallowed hard and plugged the leak. Cheerleaders don't cry unless their team loses a game.

Opa and Oma had already arrived when I got home.

"Spent the night in one of those fancy motels," Opa said chuckling. "Only problem was they didn't

101

serve breakfast until seven o'clock. Can you believe that?"

"Most folks don't get up at five A.M.," Oma said, tweaking his nose. "Glory be! Margo, you look wonderful. Cheerleading must agree with you."

"I was worried about her at first," Mom confessed. "But Dr. Jaggers says she's as healthy as a horse."

"Just not as big as one," I quipped.

Oma winked at me. I winked back. I could hardly wait to get her alone for a talk. Somehow I thought she might be able to fix everything.

"Guess what?" Mom said. "Uncle Jack, Aunt Rose, Will, and Seth are coming tomorrow! Will's bringing his wife and their new baby. Ella's the first great-grandchild."

"Be a tight squeeze," observed Opa.

"Nonsense! We can fit everyone in for one night," Mom said. "Margo, you go set up a cot in my sewing room. Jack and Rose can have your room."

"Sure," I said, putting my cheerleader smile in place. "No problem."

"As soon as you're finished come down and help Oma and me make a few extra dishes."

I tried to keep my disappointment from showing as I went upstairs to move my things. With all that crowd I'd never get a moment alone with Oma.

The three of us worked in the kitchen most of the afternoon. I think Oma might have figured something was wrong when I put the jello salad in the oven to cool and the extra pumpkin pie in the refrigerator to bake. Mom just laughed but Oma gave me a questioning look.

102

"I'm a *dummkopf!*" I said, laughing at myself, wearing another fake cheerleader smile.

There wasn't time to hear yourself think, much less talk, in the next thirty-six hours. Our house was a zoo. And it was always feeding time. Visiting a zoo can be fun. Living in one gets old very quickly. I was happy to see everyone depart Friday morning.

"I have a practice at one o'clock. Can someone take me to school and pick me up at three?"

"I'll do the honors this time," Dad said. "Your mother needs a breather."

"Don't you get a vacation like everyone else?" Opa asked.

"We're going for the State Championship. Champions don't take vacations."

Those were Miss Cole's sentiments exactly. She was really ticked because two of our squad had gone out of town. She stopped just shy of calling them traitors. I sure was glad I'd showed up. We had practice anyway. If anything, Miss C. worked us twice as hard.

I went straight up to my room when I got home. I must have fallen asleep because it was almost dark when I heard someone knocking on my door. "Come in," I called, sitting up and rubbing the sleep from my eyes.

"Did I wake you?" Oma asked.

"Just grabbing some z's before dinner. Turn on the light and come in."

"I took a little nap, too," she confessed. "Did you have a hard practice?"

"I'll say! Miss Cole was mad 'cause some of the girls were out of town. Nothing we did pleased her."

"You don't seem very happy with your wish come true."

"It isn't exactly what I thought it would be."

"For me either!" Oma said, smiling. "I still have to use my contraption and rest more than I'd like. Where does your wish go wrong?"

I shrugged. "I think it's just me that's wrong." Now that I had someone to talk with the words wouldn't come. Not the right ones.

"Why do you say that?"

"I thought once I was a cheerleader everything would be wonderful. No problems. No hassles. That I'd be the same Margo—only better. Well, I'm not the same. And I'm not better. Sometimes I don't even like myself. I have more problems now than when I was a nobody."

"So cheerleading has made you a somebody. But it's a somebody you don't like?"

"Uh-huh. That's it."

"And you are the only one with this problem?"

"I guess so. I'm always the odd girl out. No matter how hard I try I don't seem to fit in with the rest of the squad."

"Do you want to fit in?"

"I like being a cheerleader!" I exploded. "Why isn't it like I thought it would be?"

"Well, before you were on the outside looking in. Often things are different from the inside out. I know for sure that nothing is any good unless you're happy with yourself."

"It isn't fair!" I stormed, kicking a shoe under my bed. "What's the use of getting your secret wish unless it turns out like you thought it would?"

"Whoa, Margo! Kicking your shoe to kingdom come won't help," Oma said. "You might as well learn right now that things aren't always going to turn out the way you plan. You can either accept it, change it, or walk away from it. And only you can decide which course is best for you."

"I don't like any of those choices."

"Margo, Oma! Dinner's ready," Mom called.

Oma pulled herself to her feet. "I have confidence in your judgment, Margo. You'll make the proper decision when the time comes."

I was disappointed. I'd hoped Oma would come up with a neat solution to my problems. And all she'd done was throw everything back in my lap.

Chapter 12

The Last Straw

"May I see you for a minute, Margo?"

My heart jumped into my throat at Mr. Page's request. Was it about the homework? I had let Tacy copy mine several times this six weeks. It couldn't be my grades! Algebra is my best subject. I hadn't made less than an *A-* on anything.

Mr. Page waited for the room to clear while I stood by his desk, shifting from one foot to another.

He leaned back in his chair and smiled at me. "You like math, don't you, Margo?"

"Yes, sir."

"You're very good at it. I heard you helping Brad before class. Your explanations were excellent."

"Brad's just having a little trouble. He caught on quickly."

"There are several students who're having trouble in this class," Mr. Page said, running a hand through his spiky ginger hair. "That's why I wanted to talk with you. More students are having difficulty than I can help on an individual basis. How would you feel about tutoring a few of them during this review period?"

"Me?"

Mr. Page nodded. "I read in a teacher's magazine about an organization called PASS—Peers Assisting Students to Succeed. I'd like to form one at Ruffner. We don't have time this six weeks but we could start with a few students like you."

"Sure, I'd like to help. It sounds fun. What would I have to do?"

"Obviously, you don't need the time to review. You could take students who need extra help into my office and work with them during class period. After we get PASS set up we can use the study halls and even have before and after school sessions. Know any other students who're aces in any subject?"

"Jeff Johnson's a whiz with computers. Cindy Cunningham's tops in English or anything to do with writing. I could probably think of some more people with a little time."

"Good! Well, how about it? Want to start tomorrow?"

"Sure. I think it's a neat idea."

"By the way, Margo, since you like math so much, why haven't you joined the Math Club?"

"I can't. It meets on Wednesday after school. I have cheerleading practice."

"Oh. Well, I wish you could join us. I think you'd like it." There was real regret in his voice. It made me feel good.

"Is it okay if I tell some of the other kids about PASS?"

"Certainly. I trust your judgment. You can be my recruiting sergeant."

Andrea, Becca, and Cindy thought Pass was a neat idea, too. They were willing to join if Mr. Page got it started.

PASS gave me an excuse to look up Jeff. In spite of Cindy's assurances, I thought Jeff'd been avoiding me. I caught up with him before fifth period and explained Mr. Page's idea. "I told him you were a whiz with computers. I hope you don't mind."

"I don't mind. Sounds like a good idea. Let me know when this thing gets rolling."

"I will."

Jeff began to move away. I gathered every ounce of courage I possessed and blurted, "Maybe we could put our heads together and come up with some more kids who'd help. Maybe after exams . . . over a Triple Delight?"

Jeff's face lit up with that awesome smile of his. It made my heart do funny little flip-flops. "That's a super idea, Margo. Let's do it."

I ran down the hall to my next class. Boy, was I happy I'd gotten up enough nerve to talk to Jeff myself. I think things are okay between us now. What a Monday!

Miss Cole's announcement added to my joy. "Girls, the new uniforms are here. Your names are on the boxes. Try them on and let's see if they live up to our expectations."

When I put mine on and looked in the mirror I felt slender and beautiful for the very first time. I felt like a real cheerleader. What I saw in the mirror made my hard work and dieting worthwhile.

108

Marvelous Monday wasn't over. I had another first. I turned a series of cartwheels that pleased Miss Cole!

"That was perfect, Margo!" she yelled. "Do it again. Girls! Watch Margo. This is how we're going to begin our new routine."

I did another perfect series. I felt as light as a feather as I flew through the air. I landed in a perfect split. And I wasn't even dizzy!

One by one the others followed. I could tell we were going to be sensational. This routine would knock people's socks off!

Miss Cole was pleased. Pleased but still a slave driver. "We lost too much valuable time over this last break, girls," she said at the end of practice. "Particularly since *some* of you weren't here. So we're having our regular practices during exams."

There were several loud groans.

"You brought this on yourselves," she said in a steely voice. "Champions don't take vacations. Not if they want to remain at the top. We have our new uniforms. We have the routines. All that remains is the dedication. Do you have it or not?"

"Yes!"

"Good! Then hit the showers and go home and hit those books!"

"Hitting the books won't do me any good," Tacy said while we were dressing.

Brandy slipped a luscious green angora sweater over her head. "Why not? It won't kill you to study for one night."

Tacy's eyes filled with tears. "Don't be mean,

109

Brandy. Unless I ace the exam I'll fail algebra. I'll never even get to wear my new uniform."

"What do you mean, Tacy Andrews?" Brandy demanded. "You can't fail! All of our routines are based on ten girls. That's what makes us unique. You can't let us down!"

Brandy's outburst brought all the other girls crowding around.

"What's wrong?"

"Why's Tacy crying?"

"Who's letting us down?"

Brandy told them in no uncertain terms.

Everyone began making suggestions at once.

"Study all night."

"Yeah, cram."

"Get Miss Cole to talk to Mr. Page. Maybe he'll give you a few points."

"Yeah, my dad says they do it all the time for athletes. We're athletes."

"Get real! Old Stingy Ginger wouldn't give the Pope an extra point."

Over the babble I yelled, "Hey, listen up! Mr. Page isn't a heavy. He's starting a new program next six weeks—just to help students in trouble."

"That's too late for me," Tacy said.

"He's helping students this six weeks, too. Talk to him tomorrow."

"You'd better do something," Brandy warned. "You're letting all of us down."

"I will. Don't tell Miss C. Not yet," Tacy begged, hugging her new uniform to her chest.

We swore to silence, though I couldn't see why. Miss Cole was bound to find out sooner or later.

Tacy couldn't cut it in algebra by cramming all night before the exam.

"If you can come over to my house tonight I'll try to help you," I volunteered as Tacy and I walked out.

"I can't. I'm babysitting tonight," Tacy replied.

"Can't you cancel?"

"No! This lady's on my mom's bowling team. Besides, I need the money. Not everyone's as rich as Brandy," Tacy snapped.

Tacy must have talked to Mr. Page because he assigned Lynn Dalton to work with her in the library workroom. I was glad he didn't assign her to me. I didn't want to get blamed if she failed.

I assumed things were going pretty well until Tacy grabbed me as I came into school Thursday morning.

"Listen, Margo, you've got to help me," she said when we reached a secluded corner.

"What's wrong?"

"This coaching deal isn't going to work. Algebra goes in one of my ears and out the other. Might as well be Greek. I'm going to fail!"

Foolishly, I asked, "What can I do?"

Tacy's eyes glittered brightly. "You know Susan Marsh? She works in the principal's office. Well, she said Mr. Page ran off the exam yesterday. And Brandy saw him put them in his desk . . . bottom right drawer."

"So?"

"His desk in the math office," Tacy said, looking at my expectantly. "Where you are every day."

The light dawned. I felt sick to my stomach. "Y-you mean you want me t-to steal a copy of the test?"

"Why not? It would be easy. He'd never suspect you because you don't need it. That gibberish makes sense to you."

I don't think I've ever been angrier. I was even too angry to speak. I walked away from Tacy as fast as I could.

"You snobby, selfish twit!" Tacy yelled after me.

People in the halls turned and looked as I raced for the restroom. I hid in a stall until I had myself under control. I couldn't believe that Tacy actually expected me to steal—to betray Mr. Page's trust. What kind of person did she think I was? Was anything that important? And what if I did swipe that test? Would that be the end? Of course not! Math—particularly algebra—is a progressive subject. You build on a firm foundation. If the foundation is missing or shaky you can't move successfully to the next step. No, to get Tacy through algebra would require constant cheating. Once I started I'd be expected to keep it up. And for what? Just so Tacy could stay on the squad. Just so we'd have a ten member team and have a better shot at the State Championship. Or so Brandy said. And Brandy always had to win. Her father only loved winners. He'd said so at the party.

I simmered all day. And I was still stewing when I went to suit up for seventh period practice. I guess my mood must have shown because everyone avoided me. Tacy and Brandy especially. They huddled in a corner whispering to a couple of other girls. I ignored them.

By the end of the period I could definitely tell something was cooking. The other cheerleaders were shooting dirty looks at me or stopping their conversations when I approached. Mitzi and Gina actually shoved in front of me at the water fountain.

"What's going on?" I asked Lori, who was waiting her turn behind me.

A flush darkened Lori's already red face. "You wouldn't help Tacy with her math. Now poor Tacy's going to fail!"

"Yeah, poor, poor, dumb Tacy!" I said angrily—and loudly.

Needless to say, our practice session was a disaster. Sharp routines require all cheerleaders be together in mind and body. We weren't.

After forty-five frustrating minutes, Miss C. blew her whistle. "Hit the showers, girls. You stink!"

I'd decided to have it out with Tacy. But before I could catch up with her, Miss Cole grabbed my arm. "Come into my office."

I didn't have much choice. She had my arm in a death grip.

As soon as the door was shut she lit into me. "Margo, you are not a team player. I've noticed this before but I'd hoped you'd come around. But now I hear you've refused to help a sister cheerleader. This is inexcusable in my book! It's evident the rest of the squad feels the same way. Today's practice was the worst I've ever seen, thanks to you. You'd better shape up. Go home and think about your selfish behavior and what it's doing to our team. I expect an apology and a change of attitude by tomorrow."

"B-but . . ."

"I don't want to hear excuses! Just go home and think about your behavior and what you are doing to the squad."

That was the last straw! I went back to the locker room and gathered my things. Thank goodness, Brandy and Tacy had disappeared or I might really have exploded. I didn't bother showering or dressing. I just threw on my coat and left without saying a word to anyone.

I trudged home through spitting snow. The dark, blue-bellied clouds matched my mood. My tears of anger and frustration froze on my cheeks.

"You're home early," Mom said. "How was practice?"

"Lousy! I don't feel so good. I'm going up to bed."

Mom put her hand on my forehead. "You're so cold I can't tell whether you have a fever or not. You should have called me to come and get you."

I brushed past her. "I don't have a fever. Honest. I'm just tired. I'll be okay after I take a nap."

I didn't mean to be rude but one more kind, caring word from Mom would have flooded the room with tears.

I took a hot shower, put on my warm flannel nightgown, dragged my old teddy bear from the closet shelf, and crawled into bed. Bear has listened to a lot of my problems and soaked up a bathtub full of my tears.

When Mom came up a few minutes later I pretended to be asleep. I didn't want to talk with anyone until I had things sorted out in my head.

Strangely enough, I wasn't angry anymore. I was coldly calm as I recalled Oma's words. I had to

114

accept the situation, try to change it, or walk away. It was as simple and as logical as that.

"Okay, Bear, listen up," I murmured. "I have this problem and three ways to solve it. Option One: Accept it. Can I swallow my doubts, my guilty feelings, and my hurt pride and go on being a cheerleader? Probably. But I'm going to be miserable. Is that childish and dumb?"

Bear didn't answer. But he looked interested.

"Okay. Option Two: Can I change things? Maybe. But you know I'm more of a follower than a leader. Besides, the other girls seem to like what they're doing. And I'm never going to change Miss Cole's opinion of me or her direction. We aren't out there to cheer for our teams anymore. We're out to win the State Championship. That isn't my idea of what being a cheerleader is all about.

"And even if, by some miracle, we did change directions, do I want to spend all of my time with a bunch of people who think I'm a selfish, stuck-up twit?"

Bear looked extremely skeptical.

"That leaves Option Three: Walk away. Bear, can I give up my secret wish—my dream? Can I go back to being a nobody? Is it better to be a happy nobody or a miserable somebody?"

I hugged Bear and ducked under the covers as I heard my brothers coming upstairs. I could tell they were trying to be quiet. But they sounded like a herd of muffled buffaloes! It made me want to giggle. I love those guys. I want them to be proud of me.

When the coast was clear I popped back out.

"Okay, Bear. I know I haven't talked to you much lately but how do I get out of this mess? That is, supposing I choose Option Three. Let's see ... I could eat my way out. I know if I turned back into a butterball blimp Miss C. would kick me off the team. ... I could fail a subject. Then Mr. Zale would kick me off. ... Or I could simply resign. There's still time to train someone to take my place."

Bear rejected my first two choices without hesitation. So did I. Why should I be fat or a dummy just because I'd made a mistake?

I got out of bed and put on my new uniform. Looking back at me in the mirror was this terrific girl. A leader. Ruffner's representative. A girl who had it made. A future State Champion. The trouble was, I didn't like her. Was that important?

I took off the uniform and crawled back into bed. I waited until dinner was over and my brothers had come tiptoeing back upstairs. Then, taking a deep breath, I went downstairs to talk to Mom and Dad.

They were just settling down in front of the TV to watch the evening news.

"I want to resign from the cheerleading squad."

Dad clicked the TV off. He and Mom exchanged glances. "That's a big decision," he said. "Want to tell us why?"

"I'm not happy. It isn't fun anymore."

"We've noticed your unhappiness," Mom said. "Is there any particular reason?"

I had decided not to burden them with the whole story. "Not really. It's a whole bunch of stuff. I don't have what it takes to be a champion. If I resign now they'll have time to train a new girl before the

116

March competition. I hope you aren't too disappointed in me."

"Never!" Dad said.

Mom's face was full of compassion. "This must be very difficult for you, Margo. You've worked very hard. I think there's more to this than you're telling us."

"What is it, Dumpling? You look so miserable."

Their love and concern broke the dam. Words and tears tumbled out. I told them everything—except about the party and my embarrassing departure. "That's it," I finished, sniffing noisily. "Helping my sister cheerleaders is one thing. Stealing a test is something else."

Dad looked at me and shook his head. "Cheating is just as wrong as stealing, Margo."

"I didn't cheat. Tacy did."

"You called it helping. But when you let Tacy copy your homework and turn it in as her own, you were cheating just as much as she was," Dad said.

Mom nodded.

"Well, I didn't feel good about doing it but I don't think it's as bad as stealing."

"In my opinion it is," Dad said. "It's the same way at the plant. If one of my men is cheating on his time card—even if he badly needs the extra money—and I know about it and don't report him, then I'm as guilty as he is of cheating the company. That's just as bad as if he were stealing parts of equipment."

"But Miss Cole said we had to help each other in every way, big or small. Everyone knows school's easy for me."

117

"And you wanted your sisters to like you," Mom said sympathetically. "You were caught between a rock and a hard place. I understand. But do you really think Miss Cole meant for you to cheat?"

"I don't know! She always looks straight at me when she talks about helping each other. She's dead set on us winning the State Championship."

"Then I'm happy you're resigning from the squad," Mom said. "But I think you ought to tell Miss Cole the reason. She should know exactly what you've done and why."

"I agree," Dad said.

"Do I have to fink on Tacy? Can't I just resign?"

"You can't confess your part without telling about Tacy, can you?"

"I could try. I think Tacy should do her own confessing. I believe Miss Cole knows anyway."

"Don't sit in judgment, Margo," Dad warned. "Miss Cole may just be an over zealous young coach who doesn't realize how her instructions are being taken."

"All right," I said with a sigh. "Are you going to punish me for cheating?"

Mom put her arm around me and squeezed. "I think giving up cheerleading is enough punishment. Do you want me to come to school with you tomorrow? To see Miss Cole, I mean."

"No. I'll do this myself. Everyone's going to think I'm crazy, you know. I'm probably the only girl in the whole world who has voluntarily resigned from a cheerleading squad."

Mom looked at me with an odd, misty light in her eyes. "You really are growing up, Margo. We'll have to remember that." There was pride and a little sadness in her voice.

Chapter 13

Truth or Consequences

I placed the neatly wrapped package on Miss Cole's desk. "I'm resigning from the squad. Here's my uniform."

Miss Cole raised one delicate eyebrow. Then she smiled. "Please shut the door, Margo."

On wobbly legs, I complied.

"Have a seat. Let's talk this over. You're not angry because of a little personal criticism, are you?"

"No, ma'am. That isn't . . ."

"Well, I should hope not! No one's perfect, Margo. You're very bright but you must learn to help those who are less fortunate academically. Now, pick up your uniform and run along to class. We'll forget all about this little episode."

She didn't believe me! I stood up and said firmly, "I don't want to be a cheerleader any longer."

Miss Cole looked as if I'd clobbered her with a baseball bat. "Are you serious?"

"Yes, ma'am. And I want to tell you . . ."

"You'd spoil our chances for the State Championship because of some ego trip?"

"That isn't true! The reason I . . ."

"I don't want to hear your excuses." Her eyes brimmed with tears. "Get out of my office."

I backed toward the door. "Can I just tell you why?"

"OUT!"

I went down the hall as fast as my rubbery legs would carry me. I was scared. I'd never seen an adult fall apart like that. I'd tried to tell her my reasons. She wouldn't listen. What was I supposed to do now?

What I wanted to do was go home. Instead I had to face the friends gathered around our lockers.

"I've resigned from the cheerleading squad," I announced and braced myself for a barrage of questions.

"You're kidding!"

"Say what?"

"Why?"

"I'll bet it has something to do with Brandy," Cindy said.

"I just wasn't happy. Cheerleading takes too much time. I wanted to do some other things."

"Like what?" Helen asked unbelievingly.

"Like PASS, the Math Club, maybe the Drama Club. And spending more time hanging out with you guys—to name only a few."

"I smell a story in this," Cindy said. "We've got to talk."

Cindy's a reporter for the school paper this year. A good one, too. She's always on the lookout for news. "This is no big deal, Cindy," I said quickly. "They can train another girl before March."

"Hah! I never knew of anyone giving up cheerleading without a good reason," Helen said.

"I think my reasons are good ones." I felt bad because I knew Helen really wanted to be on the squad.

Fortunately, the bell rang and ended our discussion.

By lunchtime the whole school was buzzing with the news. I felt that if I heard the question "Why?" one more time I'd scream.

"I still bet Brandy was at the bottom of this," Cindy said, plunking her tray down beside mine. "How come she always gets away with murder?"

"Can we please talk about something else?"

My friends had circled around me, protecting me from the questions and curious stares of others. "You got it," Cindy said. "Who has some ideas for the next issue of the paper?"

The part of the day I really dreaded was PE class. I had to face all nine cheerleaders and Miss Cole.

It was worse than I imagined. The cheerleaders gathered at one end of the locker room, laughing and talking loudly, and the rest of the class huddled together at the other end. I was in the middle—totally ignored. Even when the squad left the room no one came near me.

To make matters worse, I didn't have a regulation gym suit. I wore my practice shorts and T-shirt and stood out like a sore thumb.

A year ago I would have flooded the gym with tears. Today I hung a cheerleader smile on my face

and played basketball. I think the Wagner Waterworks has closed up shop for good.

After class Miss Fitz tapped me on the shoulder.
A look of approval was on her face. "You can get
your gym suit after exams, Margo. Size ten?"

"Thanks. I take an eight."

"You've changed a lot in a year's time."

"Yes, ma'am."

Mom wanted to march down and have it out with
Miss Cole when I told her what had happened.

"Let's wait and see how things shake down," Dad
advised. "Give tempers time to cool. You did your
part, Margo. Or tried anyway."

I was glad it was Friday. I'd have the whole
weekend to get my head together before exams.

Saturday morning I finished my chores and was
helping Mom bake when the phone rang. "I'll get it.
Hello, Wagner residence. Margo speaking."

"Hi, Margo," Jeff said. "Why so formal?"

I giggled. "That's the way Dad insists we answer.
What's up?"

"Nothing much. You studying for exams?"

"Not yet. I'm helping Mom make strudel."

"What's that?"

"The best dessert you ever tasted. It's a thin pastry
stuffed with fruit—apples today—and baked. Aren't
you working at the store today?"

"Dad let me off to study for exams. But I'm not in
the mood. Want to go to High's for a Triple Delight
this afternoon?"

"Sure. Let me check with Mom." I was amazed at
how calm I sounded—like boys asked me out all the

time. Mom surprised me even more by saying yes without giving me the third degree.

"It's okay, Jeff. Want me to meet you at High's?"

"No, I'll be by for you around one."

Promptly at one o'clock Jeff rang our doorbell. "Hi. Come on in. I'll get my coat," I said, sneaking a peek to see if he had a bike or something.

Jeff caught me. "I came on the bus," he said, giving me one of his heart-melting smiles. "We have fourteen and a half minutes to get over to Monroe Street and catch the bus on the return run."

"How do you know that?"

"Easy. I got the timetables and worked it out on my computer."

"That's great! You have just enough time to meet my folks and have a piece of strudel," I said, leading him into the den.

Jeff liked both.

We made it over to Monroe Street with time to spare. And, though I had some reservations about showing up at the favorite middle school hangout, we had a great time. Jeff obviously didn't give a hoot whether I was a cheerleader or not.

Silly me, I thought the worst was over. My reviewing went well Sunday. Monday morning exams weren't too difficult. Even the cold shoulders and steely stares I got from some girls didn't hurt too much. I wasn't looking forward to seventh period PE though.

As it turned out, I didn't have PE. Miss Fitz was waiting for me outside the girls' locker room. "Mr.

Zale wants to see you in his office, Margo. You're excused from class."

I had a sinking feeling in the pit of my stomach as I went, ever so slowly, to the principal's office.

"Go right in, Margo. Mr. Zale's expecting you," Mrs. Anderson said. Her face was grim.

Mr. Zale didn't look happy either. "Have a seat, Margo. I hear you've resigned from the cheerleading squad."

"Yes, sir."

"Would you tell me why?"

My mouth felt full of chalk dust. I cleared my throat. "Uh . . . well . . . cheerleading takes so much time. . . . There are other things I want to do . . . like PASS, Math Club . . . maybe Drama Club . . ."

Mr. Zale waited patiently.

I licked my lips and thought about what Dad had said about cheating. "No, sir. The real reason I left was because I was cheating. I don't want to cheat anymore."

"How were you cheating, Margo?"

"I let other people use my homework, outlines, and reports. I thought I was helping but it didn't feel right."

"Why did you do it then? Did anyone ask you specifically to do this?"

This was the sticky part. "Not exactly. Some of the cheerleaders asked for stuff when they'd been sick or something. Miss Cole told us to help each other in every way possible. Everyone had to stay on the team if we wanted to be State Champions. I guess it just kinda happened."

124

"I see. Do you know anything about Mr. Page's missing algebra exam?"

I could feel the blood drain from my head. The office slipped sideways. Suddenly Mr. Zale was beside my chair. "Put your head down, Margo. Mrs. Anderson, bring a glass of water!"

The office righted itself. "I'm okay," I said after I gulped a whole glass of water.

Mr. Zale pulled a chair up beside mine. "Are you certain you're all right?"

I nodded.

"Then let me tell you that Tacy and Brandy have already confessed to stealing a copy of Mr. Page's test. Tacy worked the problems at home and turned the exam in today. Mr. Page noticed that her work didn't add up to the right answers and questioned her. What do you know about this?"

"They . . . she asked me to steal it last Thursday," I said, gulping for air.

"You refused. And rather than let the squad down you resigned?"

"Yes, sir," I whispered.

"Did you tell Miss Cole your reason?"

"I tried to! She wouldn't let me. She was so angry."

Mr. Zale roughly raked a hand over his face. "I see. Tell me something, Margo. What's the difference between doing someone's work for them and giving that person the advantage of working a test at home?"

"St-stealing's out and out wrong!" I sputtered. Mr. Zale just looked at me with big, sorrowful brown eyes. "Okay, I guess there isn't any difference. I was wrong."

"Yes, you were—in several ways. You hurt yourself by doing something you felt was wrong. You hurt your teachers because they couldn't measure how well they were teaching. You were unfair to the rest of your classmates. They had to do their own assignments—busy, sick, or not. And you hurt the ones you meant to help because they didn't learn the material. Do you understand what I'm saying, Margo?"

Oh boy, did I ever! "Yes, sir. I never meant to hurt anyone. I'm sorry. I guess my heart was in the right place but my head wasn't."

An understanding smile crept over Mr. Zale's face. "I think so. Now, I want you and your parents to come to a meeting here tonight at seven o'clock. And you are not to talk with anyone about what we've discussed. Understand?"

"I won't say anything. But, Mr. Zale, my parents already know why I quit."

Mr. Zale looked sad. "This meeting is very important. Something is very, very wrong at Ruffner. I want everyone concerned with cheerleading to be here."

The intercom on the desk buzzed.

"Yes, Mrs. Anderson?"

"Miss Cole is here."

"Very well. Margo, you may go. I'll see you at seven tonight."

I swallowed hard and nodded.

"I hear you have two of my girls," Miss Cole said, breezing into the office as I opened the door.

I felt lower than a worm but I didn't think I was invisible! "I'm going home," I told Mrs. Anderson.

126

She was so upset she didn't challenge my leaving school fifteen minutes early.

As I left I saw Brandy and Tacy sitting in the office detention room. They looked more miserable than I felt.

Chapter 14

All's Well That Ends Well

Mom, Dad, and I found seats in the back of the crowded conference room. Mr. Zale, Miss Cole, and Mrs. Anderson, with her note pad, sat at a table down front.

Mr. Zale stood up. "I believe everyone concerned is present now. I've called you here tonight because something has gone very, very wrong at Ruffner Middle School. On one hand, we have the best squad of cheerleaders we've ever had. Under adverse conditions, Miss Cole and these ten girls have produced a team of championship caliber. On the other hand, several parents have called me about the emphasis placed on cheerleading, one girl has resigned from the squad, and two girls have been suspended for stealing an exam. Something is definitely amiss here."

A low buzz ran through the crowd.

Mr. Zale continued, "I realize what an honor and privilege it is to be a cheerleader. Cheerleaders are an important part of this—or any—school. But not the most important part. Our mission is to educate young minds. Everything else—football, basketball, debate, drama, band, and cheerleading—is extracurricular. I believe we've lost sight of our mission here. I take part of the blame. It's my job to know what's going on in this school. I wasn't on top of this situation. Undue pressure, cheating, and stealing have no place in education. Not even to win State Championships."

Miss Cole's face was turning from bright pink to angry red. "May I say something?"

Mr. Zale nodded and sat down.

Miss Cole looked at the audience, her chin tilted defiantly. "When Mr. Zale hired me he said he wanted Ruffner to be the best school in the state. I believed him. Our squad has worked extremely hard. We've given Ruffner a shot at the State Championship. Yes, there have had to be sacrifices. Yes, I asked the girls to help one another. But *never* did I ask them to cheat or steal."

She sat down and everyone began talking at once. Mr. Wine's voice rose above the clamor. "I hold you responsible, Miss Cole. My name has been disgraced and my daughter suspended. I intend to bring this matter up with my friends on the school board."

"Tell him, girls!" Miss Cole screeched. "How many of you think I used undue pressure? How many think I approved of any method other than studying to stay on the squad? Stand up and be counted."

Very slowly, I got to my feet. I felt naked and vulnerable with everyone looking at me. But I stood there anyway and stared Miss Cole straight in the eye. One by one, six other girls rose in the now-silent room.

Miss Cole's face crumpled. "Oh, my God," she whispered and ran from the room.

Mr. Wine grabbed Brandy's arm and dragged her up the aisle.

Brandy was crying. "Please don't send me back to Rutledge Hall. I'll be good. Please, Daddy."

The way he looked at Brandy made my blood run cold. I felt sorry for her. Miss Cole, too.

Mom squeezed my hand. "That took courage, Margo."

The rest of the meeting was a blur. I know the squad was re-organized under Miss Fitz. But mostly I sat there, thankful of my parents' love and support, wanting to go home.

When I walked into the school the next morning I knew the story was out. Students were gathered into little clusters, talking in whispers. Several people gave me strange looks as I hurried to my locker.

Andrea, Becca, Cindy, and Helen were waiting for me. "Have you heard?" Helen whispered.

"Heard what?"

Everyone began talking at once.

"Brandy and Tacy were kicked off the squad."

"For stealing a copy of Mr. Page's exam."

"They're suspended!"

"Brandy's being sent to a private school."

"No more intoxicating Brandy Wine."

"Miss Cole has been transferred to another school. They're giving her another chance because she's so young—this is her first teaching job out of college."

"How did you find out all this?" I demanded.

Becca blushed. "Mrs. Anderson lives next door to me. She was so upset after the meeting that she came over to talk to Mom. I listened."

"Does everybody know?"

"Not about the pinched exam," Cindy answered. "Everyone's discussing the change of sponsors. See, Mr. Zale called a meeting of all the parents, cheerleaders, and Miss Cole after Mr. Page found out who stole his exam and why. Seems there was a whole lot of cheating going on in—"

"I know," I interrupted. "I was there. I'm one of the cheaters."

"You?" Cindy sputtered. "I don't believe it."

This was harder than telling my parents or Mr. Zale. "It's true. I didn't steal an exam but I let some of the squad copy my homework and reports for two six-weeks. That's cheating."

"I told you you were too nice for your own good," Helen said.

"But that's not really cheating," Cindy protested.

"Yes, it is. Think about it. What if we were in the same class and I always did your homework."

Cindy grinned. "I'd sure make better grades."

"What would you do on tests? Would it be fair to Becca, Andrea, and Helen if they were in our class, too?"

"Yeah, I see what you mean," Andrea said.

"What are they going to do to you?" asked Becca.

"Mr. Zale says I can't take part in any extracurricular activities for six weeks."

"No Hops? No parties? No clubs?"

"Not even PASS," I said with real regret.

"I'll bet you could get back on the squad after your suspension's over," Helen said.

I shook my head. "I don't want to be a cheerleader anymore. Why don't you try out, Helen? There are three spots open now."

"Yeah!" Becca said. "You looked good at tryouts."

Helen beamed. "Maybe I will."

Someone tapped me on the shoulder. I turned and looked up into Jeff's face. "I got us a couple more recruits for PASS," he said. "We'll hold the fort till you can come aboard."

A big lump lodged in my throat. "Maybe Mr. Page won't want me now."

Jeff grinned. "Wrong, Margo. He sent the message. And I'll keep you filled in on our progress . . . for a price."

"What's your price?"

"A big piece of your mom's strudel for every report."

I grinned so wide I thought my face might split. "I think that can be arranged. Thanks, Jeff."

"We're going to be real busy. There'll be lots of reports," he warned, strolling away.

"Good!"

I turned back to the discussion that was still going full blast.

"Well, one good thing's come out of this mess," Cindy said. "No more Brandy and her dirty tricks."

"I feel sorry for her," I said.

"Good golly, Miss Molly! Why? I can see feeling sorry for Tacy. She has to stay and face the music. Brandy gets home free," Cindy stormed.

I shook my head. "I don't think so, Cindy. Brandy's being sent away to a school she hates. Worse than that, her parents don't love her. No matter what she does it doesn't seem to please them. Mr. Wine made that pretty clear."

"No wonder her head's messed up," Andrea said.

"That's awful!" Helen exclaimed.

"Yeah, that's the pits," agreed Cindy.

"Miss Cole's the one I feel sorry for," Becca said. "She just wanted Ruffner to be number one. Brandy and Tacy sure shot her down."

"Wa-a-it a minute." I said. "Don't blame everything on Brandy, Tacy, or the squad. Miss Cole let the air out of her own balloon. She's partly to blame for what happened. She put cheerleading above anything and everything. She pushed us to be champions no matter how we did it. I for one couldn't handle the pressure."

"You weren't the only one," Cindy said in my defense.

First bell rang and we grabbed our books and headed for class. Cindy followed me down the hall. "Are you sorry you became a cheerleader?"

"No way. My wish came true even if it didn't turn out like I thought it would. I learned a lot about other people and myself. Now I'm back to being plain old Margo again."

"Not so, Margo," Cindy said, skittering ahead of me. "You've changed. You'll never be plain old Margo again."

Cindy's words jolted me. Glory be! She was right. I had changed. I may not be Margo Wagner, spirit leader, smiley person, and State Champion, but neither was I Margo Wagner, the out-of-shape, timid, face-in-the-crowd push-over. Something good had come from my secret wish after all!

I walked into my homeroom with a genuine smile on my face.